KU-596-970

"I thought you were avoiding me."

"How could I avoid you when you were sitting right next to me?" He chuckled, but she heard the tightness in the sound.

"It sure seemed like you were trying."

There was a long silence, and then the sound of his boots on the wood floor. "I didn't want people to get the wrong idea."

She got the feeling he wasn't telling the whole truth, but she wasn't sure she wanted to hear it anyway. "And what idea is that?"

"That we're...you know. Together."

Would that really be so bad? She bit back the words. Maybe she'd been wrong about everything today. Maybe the look on his face at the church had just been surprise and not... She thought for a minute. Not what? Attraction? Desire? Boy, she'd really gotten swept up in it, hadn't she? Sure, he'd told her she looked beautiful—but wasn't he sort of obligated to say that? His behavior at dinner told the true story. Even if there was something—she'd felt it when their hands brushed—Clay would never admit it.

Dear Reader

Sometimes it takes a while for characters to get their story. When Clay Gregory strolled into ONE DANCE WITH THE COWBOY and warned Andrew to be good to Jen, I knew he was Hero Material. What I didn't realise was how hard it would be to find him the right woman. You see, I couldn't just come up with a heroine-to-order and make her fit. I tried. A few times, actually. But nothing was coming together right and I went on to write other books.

But Clay's a bit stubborn. And all the while I was writing other stories he was waiting, sometimes not so patiently, for his turn. Finally I realised the problem was that I had been looking for love in all the wrong places, as the song goes. Clay didn't need a woman to breeze into Larch Valley and sweep him off his feet. He needed to see what was right in front of him all along.

I'm so pleased that you're finally going to read Clay and Meg's story. As always, I love hearing from readers, so please drop by my website at www.donnaalward.com, or contact me through my publisher.

Best wishes and happy reading!

Donna

HOW A COWBOY STOLE HER HEART

BY
DONNA ALWARD

All the characters in this book have no existence outside the imagination of the author, and have no relation whatsoever to anyone bearing the same name or names. They are not even distantly inspired by any individual known or unknown to the author, and all the incidents are pure invention.

All Rights Reserved including the right of reproduction in whole or in part in any form. This edition is published by arrangement with Harlequin Enterprises II BV/S.à.r.l. The text of this publication or any part thereof may not be reproduced or transmitted in any form or by any means, electronic or mechanical, including photocopying, recording, storage in an information retrieval system, or otherwise, without the written permission of the publisher.

® and TM are trademarks owned and used by the trademark owner and/or its licensee. Trademarks marked with ® are registered with the United Kingdom Patent Office and/or the Office for Harmonisation in the Internal Market and in other countries.

First published in Great Britain 2011
by Mills & Boon, an imprint of Harlequin (UK) Limited,
Eton House, 18-24 Paradise Road, Richmond, Surrey TW9 1SR

© Donna Alward 2011

ISBN: 978 0 263 22119 0

Harlequin (UK) policy is to use papers that are natural, renewable and recyclable products and made from wood grown in sustainable forests. The logging and manufacturing process conform to the legal environmental regulations of the country of origin.

Printed and bound in Great Britain
by CPI Antony Rowe, Chippenham, Wiltshire

A busy wife and mother of three (two daughters and the family dog), **Donna Alward** believes hers is the best job in the world: a combination of stay-at-home mum and romance novelist. An avid reader since childhood, Donna always made up her own stories. She completed her Arts Degree in English Literature in 1994, but it wasn't until 2001 that she penned her first full-length novel and found herself hooked on writing romance. In 2006 she sold her first manuscript, and now writes warm, emotional stories for The Cherish™ Series.

In her new home office in Nova Scotia, Donna loves being back on the east coast of Canada after nearly twelve years in Alberta, where her career began, writing about cowboys and the West. Donna's debut Romance, HIRED BY THE COWBOY, was awarded the Booksellers Best Award in 2008 for Best Traditional Romance.

With the Atlantic Ocean only minutes from her doorstep, Donna has found a fresh take on life, and promises even more great romances in the near future!

Donna loves to hear from readers. You can contact her through her website at www.donnaalward.com, her page at www.myspace.com/dalward, or through her publisher.

WOLVERHAMPTON PUBLIC LIBRARIES	
XB000000125081	
Bertrams	24/10/2011
- 5 NOV 2011	£13.50
CO☒H	01379113

To the beautiful, brave survivors everywhere.
You are amazing.

CHAPTER ONE

CLAY GREGORY stood in the middle of the barn corridor, his booted feet planted on the cold concrete and his hands shoved into the pockets of his sheepskin jacket. His breath formed frosty clouds in the air and his dark eyes glittered beneath the brown knitted hat he wore in lieu of his customary Stetson.

Meg looked away, determined to ignore him. Clay Gregory thought himself a cut above and she didn't mind taking him down a peg or two this cold March morning. She refused to glance his way again, instead giving her shovel a satisfying scrape along the stall floor. She dumped the soiled straw into a waiting wheelbarrow. She made the same action twice more, each time her heart thumping a little harder as he remained silent. The increase in her heart rate wasn't from the physical exertion, though the exercise was a welcome feeling after months of *taking it easy*.

Nope. The hammering pulse was one hundred percent caused by Clay. The last time he'd spoken to her it had been to accuse her of running away. She'd wanted to make him understand, but his mind had been closed. The spectre of cancer had killed most of her romantic illusions where Clay was concerned, and his harsh words had finished the job. She'd told herself she was over her

schoolgirl crush, but his censure had bothered her more
than she cared to admit. Because there wasn't just a crush
at stake. They'd been friends first, and the words he'd
flung at her had hurt more than he knew.

"Megan."

Finally. His deep voice seemed to fill the corridor and
she took a measured breath. She stood the shovel on its
blade and rested her hands on the handle as she looked
up, meeting his gaze dead-on. "Hello, Clay."

He took a step forward. Meg gripped the shovel handle and stepped back, resuming her task. She had to keep
working. She didn't want to talk to Clay, not this morning. Facing things one at a time was what she intended
to do and Clay Gregory's closed mind was not on the list
for today.

"You're back," he said, and she realized he was only
a few feet behind her.

"Yes, I'm back. Thanks for noticing."

"I came looking for Dawson."

Oh, so he wasn't here to see her after all. She bit down
on her lip to keep from blurting out the sharp reply that
had formed in her head. There was no reason for her pride
to be hurt. Clay had said some very painful things last
spring. When he'd accused her of running away he was
right. She had been, but her reasons had been solid. At
least to her. She made the best decision she could and she
didn't regret it one bit. She was here now because she'd
made the decision to fight with all she had. If Clay didn't
like it that was his problem.

"We had some problems with calves last night," she
said blandly. "Dawson went back to bed and I said I'd do
the horses."

She didn't need to look at Clay to know he was scowling. He had a way of frowning that made a line form be-

tween his eyebrows. When she'd still been able to tease him she'd called it a penny slot, and many a time she'd wanted to smooth the crease away but she'd been too chicken to touch him in such an intimate manner.

She'd save herself that humiliation, thank you very much. The only thing worse than having a crush on her brother's best friend while growing up had been the possibility of acting on it and being rejected. As she surely would have been. Clay had never shown the slightest interest in her *that way*. He'd always treated her like an annoying little sister.

"Give me the shovel," he said, and his long arm reached around and closed over hers on the black handle.

Megan ignored the automatic zing that raced down her limbs at the contact and pulled the implement out of his grasp. "What are you doing?"

His response was to grip her shoulders and turn her around.

She looked up—a long way up, because Clay was over six feet tall and she came in at a measly five foot five. She couldn't help the thrill that coursed through her at his nearness.

Coursed through every part of her body, save one. On the right side of her chest she felt nothing, because there was nothing there.

This was so not how it was supposed to go. Clay Gregory *and* the cancer were in the past. She wished she could just forget about them both. But both had left their indelible mark no matter how hard she tried to move past them.

"What was Dawson thinking, letting you do this?" he demanded, the line between his brows now a deep crater above his nose.

She pulled away and lifted her chin. Not like it would

make her any taller, but it made her feel better. "Dawson doesn't *let* me do anything. He's not the boss of me."

Great. That made her sound what, ten years old? She glared at him as best she could. She hadn't come back to Larch Valley just so people could start bossing her around and treating her with kid gloves. "I've been mucking out stalls since I was a kid, Clay. If you want to see Dawson, he's up at the house. Let me get back to work."

Her snappish words seemed to take him back a bit as the line eased but the concern still rested heavy in his eyes. "Are you sure you should be doing heavy labor, Meg? You shouldn't do too much and…"

"And what?" she finished for him. What did he think would happen? There were no more stitches to pop. She wasn't going to collapse at his feet. "Shoveling…you-know-what is hardly heavy labor. I think I know what I can and can't handle," she replied, but she softened her tone a bit. There was no sense in arguing. "I'm fine, Clay. I'm all better now. Good as new."

It was a lie, but it would be truth soon enough. Granted, there were still lingering issues since her treatment. Twinges that happened at the oddest times. Fatigue. Then there was the issue of her scars. They would never go away, but the rest would be cured by time and working to get stronger. "Farm work is exactly what I need."

Megan Briggs had been just about as low as she ever cared to get, but that was over now. Breast cancer hadn't beaten her—she'd beaten it. Now it was time to reclaim her life. She had ideas—good ones. And if she wanted her family's support, she had to first prove to them that she wasn't going to fall apart at any moment. They needed her. And while the past year couldn't have been helped, she was determined to help keep the Briggs ranch on its feet.

If people kept tiptoeing around her like she was break-able, how on earth was she ever going to make it happen? But she wasn't about to give up. And so she tightened her hands around the shovel, prepared to resume her work.

Clay's response was to retrieve another shovel from beside the door. Megan looked up at him and wasn't sure if she was flattered or insulted at his obvious caring. She decided insulted. It was easier that way.

"I can do this," she repeated, feeling a silly urge to stamp her foot. She did not. She merely stared at him as he took the stall next to her and dug in. "Clay! I said I've got it."

"Shut up, Meg," he said mildly, igniting her temper even further.

It would serve him right if she walked out and let him do them all, she thought. But that wouldn't help her cause one little bit. She needed everyone to see she was fine. Same old Meg. Reliable and ready to put in a hard day's work. Not a burden. Not a girl who needed to be pampered. Definitely not made of glass, ready to break at any moment. That whole "poor Meg" bit was what had driven her to Calgary in the first place.

"Fine." She wasn't about to stand and argue about it. She finished the stall she was on and moved the barrow down the aisle, beginning on another. A raw breeze blew through the door at the end of the barn, and when Meg looked up, soft flakes were falling. The horses were hud-dled together in the corral, the light snow dusting their backs.

The hard edge of her mood melted away and she smiled to herself. The horses, this ranch, her family—they were what were important now. She had to remember that. She'd done what she had to do to get through her illness, but oh, it was wonderful to be home. This was where she belonged. And where she would stay.

Clay saw the hint of a smile touch Meg's face and some of his frustration mellowed. It was good to have her back. Good to see her looking so well. A little thinner than he remembered, but with the same thickly lashed, saucy brown eyes and the same dusting of freckles over her nose. She wore a horribly ugly hat on her head that looked like it had been knitted by yarn odds and ends, the colors varied and mismatched.

It suited her to a T. Meg had always been a little unconventional and he'd liked that about her. When she'd snapped at him her delicate features had taken on a familiar stubborn set. Meg had never cared what other people thought. That was what made her disappearance to Calgary so troubling. Suddenly the spunky girl he'd always known had turned into a frightened waif running away. He'd been worried and had gone about telling her in all the wrong ways.

Now she was back and he *wanted* to believe she was okay. She certainly looked fine. She'd told him she'd be back strong and fit and he'd had his doubts. Doubts he'd refused to voice, because he'd been afraid. He'd admitted it to no one but himself. He'd been afraid Meg was going to die. The girl in dark, curly pigtails who had held his hand in hers and said she'd always be there for him had faced something that made promises irrelevant.

And instead of talking about it he'd lashed out. What he *had* said all those months ago had been so very wrong and he'd regretted those words ever since. Dawson had mentioned she was coming home and Clay had thought to catch his friend in the barns, do a little digging about her state of mind—and health—before facing her again.

Instead of Dawson he'd found Meg, cleaning stalls like the last year had never happened. He owed her an apology for those words.

"You're truly okay?" He kept shoveling, needing to keep moving, to pretend that this was like any other sort of conversation he'd had with Meg a thousand times.

Instead he found himself face-to-face with her and her sharp attitude. The sweet Megan he remembered was gone and replaced by a woman with a stubborn jut to her chin and eyes full of fire. Before he would have been able to soothe ruffled feathers with a smile and a bit of charm. But Meg seemed immune now. The words of apology he'd practiced in his head disappeared, swept away on the arctic air blowing through Larch Valley.

"I wouldn't be here if I wasn't," she replied, shaking fresh straw on to the stall floor.

He looked up briefly. She was watching him, her eyes enormous above her plaid wool jacket. Old work gloves covered her hands and she wore jeans and boots, same as him. At this moment, it was hard to imagine her body being ravaged by disease.

"If I said I was sorry for what I said to you last spring, would you believe me?" He stumbled over the words. They were nothing like he'd rehearsed, but he couldn't take them back now. What was he supposed to say? That all the hateful things he'd said had eaten at him all these months? That at the time he'd been afraid they were the last words he might ever say to her? Her current strength and determination made the sentiments seem ridiculous.

"Sure." She shook out more straw over the floor and he gritted his teeth. She was certainly as mule headed as ever.

"Do you want to talk about it?"

She looked up at him. "Not really. Let's just let it drop."

In Clay's experience, a woman never "dropped" anything, but Megan wasn't like most women. He had no idea what to say next. He'd apologized and he'd meant it. Maybe that was enough.

"Did your mom tell you about Aunt Stacy?"

With a sigh, Meg put her shovel aside. "No, she didn't. What's to know?"

"Gee, Meg, I'm sorry, is my conversation boring you?" He couldn't keep the sarcasm out of his tone. She was completely exasperating. He'd come over here, wanting to say hello, wanting to say he was sorry, and he got a sharp tongue and put-upon air for his troubles.

A slight flush touched her cheekbones and she looked a little sheepish. "Of course not. I'm a little touchy, okay? Everyone is treating me like I'm going to break at any moment. It's a bit suffocating."

"That wasn't my intention."

She raised an eyebrow and he knew she was right. It had been, from the moment he had said she shouldn't be mucking out stalls. He'd taken a heavy hand from the start. Well, sue him for being worried about her. "If people are concerned, it's only because they care about you and don't want you to do too much, too fast."

"I know that."

"You've just come home. I'm sure once everyone sees you're back to your old self, they'll move on to another topic." He made his voice sound far more confident than he felt.

Clay knew very well how the gossip in the town worked. There was a flavor of the week and then something newer and juicier came along. Hell, at his age he could hardly go out on a date without the grapevine marrying him off by the next morning. Even his aunt Stacy had gotten in on the needling a bit lately, asking if there was any particular young lady he was interested in. The answer was always an unequivocal no. Not that he would have admitted otherwise if there was someone who caught his eye.

He shut the stall door and latched it. "You were gone the better part of a year," he said. "You're still a bit of a mystery to a lot of the people of Larch Valley. It'll blow over."

When he turned back, there were tears glimmering in Meg's eyes. His stomach clenched. He didn't know how to handle a woman's tears. Not even a woman like Megan, who he'd known most of his life and who, for the most part, had been just one of the gang. He couldn't recall ever seeing her cry in his life. "Did I say something wrong?"

She shook her head, and he noticed she bit down on her lip when it started to quiver. Was there something else going on? Worry slid coldly down his spine. He was so not good with this sort of thing. Tears, sickness…these were the kinds of things he normally wouldn't touch with a ten-foot pole. Not even for Meg.

But just as soon as the emotion had bubbled to the surface, she locked it away. "I thought going away and coming back would be easier, but…" The word caught a bit and she took a breath, regaining control. The next sentence came out stronger. "But it's been more stressful than I expected. I feel like I can't do anything without being watched and examined, and that's just by Mom, Dad and Dawson."

"And now me."

"I appreciate that you care, Clay…"

But he got the picture. He was in the way. She might have accepted his apology but he suspected what he'd said still stung. Maybe it always would—he hadn't been kind. He should be relieved. After all, facing a friend with cancer hit a little too close to home for Clay's comfort. It brought back way too many bad memories. And yet, her veiled dismissal left him with a hollow feeling of disappointment.

"Hint taken." He pasted on what he figured was a polite enough smile and dusted off his hands, thumping his leather gloves together. "And your stalls are done."

"Thanks for your help."

He wasn't entirely sure if she was sincere. But he knew one thing—she was struggling. She needed her friends to rally around her. "Look, tomorrow night is our regular wing night at the Spur. Why don't you come out? Have you seen the girls yet?"

She shook her head. Something lit in her eyes that was gratifying to see, instantly followed by indecision. He pressed on. "You know Jen and Lily will be thrilled to see you. And Lucy's bound to be there with Brody if they can get a sitter." The circle of friends was tight, and he knew they'd show the support he was reluctant to give, paltry as it was. "Surely a few drinks and hot wings is a good way to start, isn't it?"

"I don't know..."

Clay's worry increased. Meg had never been a party girl, but she wasn't usually this withdrawn. She'd always sort of been there. Steady as a rock. Ready with a laugh and a smile. He set his shoulders. No disease should be allowed to take that effervescence away from her.

"You think about it," he said, in a voice that really left no room for refusal. "And if you want a drive, call me. I'll pick you up on the way by."

"I'll think about it," she replied, but in a small voice that he didn't like the sound of at all.

He nodded before spinning on his heel.

"Clay?"

He turned back at the sound of her voice. She was standing in the middle of the corridor, her gloved hands resting once again on the top of the shovel. The mishmash of work clothes should have made her unattractive, but she wasn't. Her skin was glowing in the cold air and her eyes had always been particularly pretty, dark brown and glittering with mischief.

"What about your aunt Stacy?" she called, and Clay finally grinned. The good news about his aunt never failed to bring a smile to his face.

"She's getting married," he replied, and with a wave headed out of the barn, back to his truck. "Think about it, huh," he muttered to himself as he started the engine. He was well aware that Meg's social life wasn't any of his business. She was a grown woman, certainly able to take care of herself.

But then he thought about how pale her skin looked and how she seemed to shrink at the idea of going out with friends. She needed a nudge, that was all. Tomorrow night he was stopping to get her whether she liked it or not. It was for her own good.

Yesterday had not been a good day for Clay. The calf had been delivered by cesarean and even then it had not been enough. Clay had held high hopes for this breeding pair and had paid good money for the privilege. Having the calf deliver stillborn put him in a rotten mood. By the time he'd handled things at the barn and showered, wing night was well under way when he'd arrived at the Spur and Saddle. Megan hadn't shown, either, and by the end of the night he'd been downright grouchy. He'd returned home in an even worse mood and spent a restless night tossing and turning in his bed.

Clay turned into the Briggs farmyard early the next morning with a scowl still on his face. He hadn't really expected her to come out but he'd hoped the idea of Jen and Lily being there would entice her. She couldn't stay hidden away forever. She might be back in town but she was still running away from all the people who would support her. Not that it mattered to him personally, he told himself, but the behaviour got his back up. It was weak and selfish to his mind. It reminded him of his mother and that always left a bitter taste in his mouth.

Well, he wasn't about to confront her today. He had too much weighing on his mind, including talking to Dawson about the upcoming meeting of local ranchers. He was relieved to see her car wasn't in the driveway. After bungling his apology yesterday he wasn't in any mood to cross swords. He had enough on his plate.

The barn was empty when he checked so he made his way to the house, his boots crunching on the brittle snow.

He knocked at the back porch, and when there was no answer, tried the knob. He and Dawson had been dashing in and out of each other's houses since they were old enough to run between farms, and going in to leave a note was common practice. The door was unlocked as usual and he entered the mudroom, removing his boots before stepping inside the warmth of the kitchen. It smelled like cinnamon and vanilla and his stomach rumbled. With Aunt Stacy gone most of the time now, he'd had to rely on his own basic cooking and once she was married he'd be on his own altogether. Which was fine. He wouldn't starve. But he was the first to admit he wasn't so great on the baking sweets end of things.

The coffee cake sat on a cooling rack and he imagined cutting a slice while it was still warm. He smiled to himself. Linda Briggs would give him heck if he pulled such a stunt.

Linda always kept a notepad beside the phone, too. He went to the counter and grabbed a pen.

"Clay!"

He jumped at the sound of his name, nearly dropping the pen.

Megan stood at the junction between hall and kitchen wearing jeans and a sweater and a towel wrapped around her head. She looked anything but happy to see him. "Don't you knock?"

He forced a calming breath. "Since when have we ever knocked?" He picked up the pen and began writing, trying to look far more composed than he felt. His heart was beating a mile a minute. As he scribbled the note he said, "And as a matter of fact, I did knock. No one answered."

"I was upstairs."

He looked up. She didn't wear a speck of makeup and the dark blue towel contrasted with her flawless complexion. He could smell the flowery scent of her soap or shampoo from where he stood and it felt disturbingly intimate. "So I gathered. I'll be out of your way in a minute. I'm just leaving a note for Dawson."

He finished and ripped the paper off the tablet. "Where is he, by the way?"

Megan's lips twisted and she looked away. "He didn't come home last night. And he has my car."

Clay remembered the goofy way his friend had looked at Tara Stillwell last night as she'd waited on them at the Spur. Dawson had been interested in her for weeks, but Clay hadn't realized the attraction went both ways so completely. "Tara's a nice girl. He could do worse."

"Tara...you mean Tara from my graduating class?" She finally moved from the doorway and into the kitchen.

"You didn't know?"

Megan shook her head, looking genuinely distressed. "Not a clue. He never said a word to me about it."

"I guess you haven't been here to see," Clay replied, unable to resist the slight dig.

Fire flashed in Meg's eyes as the towel slipped on her head. With a look of annoyance she took it off. "I'm well aware that I've been out of town," she snapped. "I don't know why you feel you must continue to bring it up. And my family did visit me, you know. If Dawson kept his personal life to himself, I'm not totally to blame for that, too."

Clay heard the sharp words but they bounced off him at the shock of seeing her hair. It was short, sleek and lighter than he remembered, even though it was wet. A light reddish-brown color that reminded him of Tinkerbell. Short and saucy and cute.

But it was the cause of the change that felt like lead in his feet, heavy and immovable. All her gorgeous dark curls were gone. The woman in front of him seemed even more of a stranger.

Her wide, honeyed eyes looked into his. "The chemo," she acknowledged quietly. There was no resentment in the words—just acceptance, and it damn near ripped his heart out.

"Meg." The word came out like a croak; he hadn't realized how his throat had closed over. Seeing her in boots and with a shovel in her hand had been one thing. She had been Dawson's little sister, Clay's old friend. It had been easier to pretend that there wouldn't be physical changes after what she'd been through.

But this was evidence. Proof of what she'd suffered. Proof of things changing when Clay wanted them to be the same as they'd always been. Easy. Damn, it had always been easy with Meg, right up until the time she got sick and everything changed.

"It's okay," she replied, folding the towel neatly. "It's coming back in now, it just takes some getting used to. I like it. It's easy to care for."

She smiled but he caught the wobble at the edges. For the first time ever he was glad she'd done her treatment in Calgary. Yes, she'd have had support in Larch Valley, but he wouldn't have been the man to provide it as much as he'd like to pretend otherwise. Megan was a friend and he'd wanted to be there for her, but he couldn't handle this sort of thing and he hated what that said about him.

He'd had no choice but to watch his father waste away. He'd been ten years old and there had been nowhere for him to go, no escape. He'd idolized his dad, even when the big man had been reduced to a shadow of his former self. Now Clay was torn between resenting Meg for running away and being grateful that he hadn't had to witness the harsh realities of her treatment. It was over, but just the idea of Meg being completely bald seemed unreal and made his stomach do a slow, heavy twist.

"I'd better get going." He put the note on the counter and headed back for the mudroom and his boots.

"Is it really that ugly?"

Her soft voice chased after him and he stopped, dropping his head. He couldn't leave knowing she thought… Oh hell. How women thought was far beyond him most days but he was bright enough to realize that he'd hurt her feelings by reacting the way he had. She'd lost all her hair. Megan had never been what he considered high maintenance, but he understood that she had to be feeling insecure about her appearance. He wasn't totally insensitive.

He turned back. "No," he said, the kitchen so perfectly

silent that his quiet response filled every corner. She was absolutely gorgeous if he were being honest with himself. The fact that he noticed was quite troubling. But he wouldn't deny her the words. He wasn't that cold. "It's not bad at all. You're as beautiful as you ever were."

It was the last thing he expected that would make her cry.

CHAPTER TWO

"You're as beautiful as you ever were."

The burst of emotion was so sudden and unfamiliar that Megan choked on the sob that tore from her throat. She quickly covered her mouth with her hands, but Clay was staring at her like he'd never seen her before. Megan Briggs did not cry, especially not in front of anyone. But this time she seemed unable to control her reaction. It hit too close to her heart.

Clay Gregory had just said she was beautiful. She closed her eyes and two tears slid down her cheeks. The irony hit her like a fist—she wasn't beautiful. Not any-more, not even close. For years she'd longed to hear those words from his lips, and now that she didn't want them they were offered in the bitterest of circumstances. Because she was less than whole, she was vulnerable and worst of all—needy.

She'd solicited his remark, rather than simply ac-cepting his tepid reaction to her pixie-short hair. And of course he would say that, out of duty. Out of sympathy.

Clay didn't know the changes cancer had wrought on her body and the scars it had left behind. Losing her hair was nothing in the greater scheme of things. She was missing a breast. She'd had treatments that had changed so much of her body's chemistry that things she'd barely given a passing thought to before—like one day being married and having a family—were suddenly important and very uncertain. And yet somehow she knew, deep inside, that even if Clay was only trying to make her feel better, somehow he meant the words. She gathered them close to her heart and cherished them.

"I'm sorry," she said, trying to pull the pieces of herself together. Both times she'd seen Clay since her return, she'd teared up and she didn't like that one bit. If she couldn't deal with one annoying rancher, how could she face her friends—the whole town for that matter—with a smile on her face? The last thing she wanted was to break down in public. She had *never* been a crier, but her emotions seemed harder to control these days. She couldn't just jump back into the social scene without trusting herself to hold it together first.

"I didn't mean to make you cry," he replied, shoving his hands in his pockets. He shifted his weight uncomfortably.

Great. First she'd practically forced him into paying her a compliment, and now he looked like he'd rather be anywhere than standing in her kitchen. "Don't mind me." She picked up the towel and folded it neatly to give her hands something to do. Embarrassment crept through her as she tried to explain. Honesty was probably the best approach—as honest as she was comfortable being, anyway.

"The truth is, Clay, I'm working through stuff. I know I'm not the same woman I was a year ago. I look different. I feel different." She swiped her finger under her eyes, wiping away the rest of the moisture. "Physically...there are some adjustments. Emotionally, too. But I made you uncomfortable and I'm sorry for that."

Of course she had made him uncomfortable. Talking to Clay about cancer was like chatting to a closed door—

words bounced off and there was no response. He avoided the topic whenever he could. When she'd told their circle of friends of the biopsy results, Clay had turned ashen and left the room. Cancer had stolen his father and in a way his mother, too. And if Meg knew anything about Clay from their years of friendship, it was that he handled things in one of two ways—he charmed his way through or put his shoulder to the wheel.

Since he wasn't employing his charms, Meg could only assume he was forging ahead, doing what he had to do to make the best of the situation but wearing blinders to everything negative about her illness that bothered him.

Clay's dark eyes caught hers. "I'm fine." He paused for a second and then asked, "Is that why you didn't go to the pub last night? Because you're *working through stuff?*"

She'd wanted to go. She'd actually figured out what she was going to wear and everything. But when the time came she'd been utterly exhausted. Even now that her treatment was done, fatigue continued to knock her flat without any notice. The idea of facing everyone for the first time feeling so run-down was too daunting, and besides, convincing them she was all right in such a state was laughable.

Not that she could explain it to Clay. He was already tiptoeing around her, holding himself back. She had to be one hundred percent or people would go around thinking she was sick again.

"I spent the night with Mom," she answered. "After being gone so long…"

She let the thought hang. Let Clay reach his own conclusions—that she'd caught up on some quality time with her mother. It wasn't totally untrue.

Today she was feeling much better. She'd done chores

and had breakfast and showered. The cake she'd made was nearly cool enough to eat and she still had energy to burn. She might not be ready for a night at the pub, but she was going a little stir crazy being cooped up on the ranch. She needed to get out and do something. No one else would listen to her plans. But maybe Clay would. Clay had fought against the odds himself and was always looking at ways of improving his operation.

Besides, when he left today she wanted him to remember her strong and fit and ambitious. Not with the pity she knew was hiding behind his worried eyes.

"You busy? Do you have time for a ride?"

Clay's hands came out of his pockets. "A ride?"

"I want to show you something. Besides, Clover and Calico can both use the exercise."

"I don't know. I should get back."

Meg shrugged. "Never mind then. It's not important." She was disappointed at his response. Heck, she was disappointed in him if it came down to it. After his apology the other day she'd hoped they'd get back to an easy friendship, but that didn't seem to be the case.

She expected him to leave but he didn't move. Instead he watched her with a puzzled look on his face. "I can probably spare an hour or so."

Meg forced a smile, determined to put her mini breakdown behind her. Despite his recent reticence, she knew Clay was open-minded and fair and would give her an honest opinion. "Great. I'll put on my coat and meet you in the barn."

When she joined him, he already had Clover saddled and he was laying a blanket over Calico's withers. Meg went up to the mare and gave her nose an affectionate rub. "You didn't waste any time."

"I knew which saddle was yours." He gave the saddle

a swing and settled it on Calico's back, reaching for the cinch straps.

Meg reached for a bridle, suddenly realizing how familiar they really were with each other. It was nothing for Clay to walk in here and know the stock and tack as well as his own. For all intents and purposes, he'd been like a part of the family since forever.

That had taken a serious hit when she broke the news about her illness. If he'd *truly* known her, he never would have judged her so harshly.

And yet she knew that of anyone, he would understand her plans for the future. He felt about his ranch the way she felt about the Briggs place. She put her boot in the stirrup and slid into the saddle—after years of being with Calico it was as familiar and comfortable as an easy chair. This was one thing that hadn't changed, that wouldn't change. This was who she was, she realized. And nothing—or no one—would take that away from her. Not ever again.

Full of renewed purpose, she gripped the reins in her gloved hand. "I want to show you something," she said to Clay, and with a nudge of her heels led the way out of the barn.

The bitter cold from the arctic front was being nudged away by a Chinook arch that was forming to the west. She gave the mare a little kick and they crested the rise. Meg moved fluidly into a trot, loving the feel of being on horseback again. Feeling restless, Calico gave a little kick and Meg laughed out of simple joy.

Clay caught up and she looked over at him appraisingly. Sure, maybe the juvenile crush days were over, but she had to admit he still looked pretty amazing in his black Stetson and jeans. The denim clung to his strong legs and he sat a horse as prettily as she'd ever seen. And he had called her beautiful. Not just now, but before. As beautiful as you ever *were*, he'd said. He couldn't possibly know how much of a hit her vanity had taken over the last few months. She never felt womanly or beautiful these days. It gave her badly bruised feminine pride a boost to think that even if he'd never cared for her in *that* way, he'd at least noticed her on some level.

"Snow'll be gone by morning," Clay said as they slowed. "We could use some milder weather."

"Sure makes calving a lot easier." She let herself be drawn back to practicalities.

"We lost one yesterday."

Meg turned to look at him as Calico picked her way along the familiar trail. "Oh, no."

"It happens. Pete and I did a C-section but it was too late."

"Pete's the best there is," Meg answered, knowing how Clay valued his foreman. "But no one said it was easy. There are lots of operations struggling right now." She let out a breath. It was the perfect way to lead into what she wanted to talk to him about.

"That's what I wanted to talk to Dawson about before the next meeting," he said.

"You mean us," she said faintly, rocking in the saddle as Calico started up over a knoll.

"You?"

He sounded so surprised Meg clamped her mouth shut. As close as Clay was to her family, he didn't seem to know about the troubles the Briggs's were having. It wasn't as bad as some, that's for sure. But it was enough that Meg had trouble sleeping at night wondering how they were going to make it through. If they had a bad year, the results could be devastating to their place.

She reached up and tugged her hat further over her ears.

"So what did you want to show me?"

She reined in and looked down the hill at the ranch. "That," she said, lifting her voice above the rising wind.

"It's your place. So?"

The barns were spread out over the farmyard, machinery lined up precisely, fences in good repair. Nothing, she knew, was wasted or neglected. "Dawson has done a good job, hasn't he?"

"He's a good rancher."

"It's a two-man ranch, though, don't you think?"

"Same as mine, I suppose. Though I've got Pete and some hired help in the summer."

"We don't."

Meg turned her back to the view and looked earnestly at Clay. "For a while I was the second man, remember?"

"And in the summers you did the circuit."

"That's right," she replied, remembering the long days of travel and the rush of competing in rodeos as a barrel racer. Clay was watching her closely. She wanted to share her idea with someone who could see the potential in it rather than just seeing reasons why not. "Calico and I competed. And the money I made paid my expenses and the rest went back into the ranch."

"Are you saying you want to start racing again?"

Meg thought of the rows of trophies she'd earned over the years. It had been fun and challenging and she'd been good at it. But now she wanted more. To put down roots instead of the constant travel during the season. To make her mark in a different, long-lasting way. She wanted to build something, watch it flourish, and the thrill of winning did have an expiry date.

"Not exactly. I want to do something else, Clay. More

than help with the chores and hope for the best, you know?"

She looked up at him, wanting him to understand. "I love this place. It's mine, too, as much as it is Dawson's. It's in here." She pressed her right hand to her heart. "But yeah, we're struggling. And the whole damn family is treating me with kid gloves and won't even listen to my ideas!"

The last part came out with a little more vitriol than she expected and she saw Clay's lips twitch.

"Meg." His tone was patronizing and it set her teeth on edge. "You've only just come home. Maybe you need to give it time. Wait until you're better."

That was what her mother had said. And her dad. And Dawson. She glared up at him. She had expected a better response from everyone, and they kept letting her down. Meg had always been the reliable one. Always the one who took on the burdens of the family and held things together. She knew that and accepted it. Everyone thought she'd run away to Calgary for treatment but she'd really gone because it was best for the family. All she was trying to do was make things better again, to make up for the time she'd been gone. She knew she'd left them in a bind and carried her own bit of guilt about it, even as she knew there was nothing she could have done to prevent it.

"I *am* better," she insisted. "I thought talking to you might be different. I thought you'd understand, but I guess not." She gave the reins a jerk and wheeled away, pushing Calico into a canter over the frozen prairie.

She heard his shout behind her but the wind was in her face now and it felt glorious. They could all go hang as far as she was concerned! Hooves pounded on the solid ground, sending up a familiar rhythm. Right now she felt as if she could ride for days. The air burned deliciously in her lungs. She'd needed this so badly.

Clay blew out a breath of frustration as Megan took off. Why did she take everything he said in the wrong way? He urged Clover to hurry the pace as they followed Meg and Calico up over the butte. He'd only wanted her to try looking at it from her family's side. They were afraid for her.

Heck, he was afraid for her. She looked wonderful, said all the right assurances. But he still had his doubts that everything would be as okay as she insisted. And that niggling bit of doubt scared the hell out of him.

He drew up alongside of Calico and rather than try to stop her, he kept pace. Megan was the most stubborn woman he knew—next to his aunt Stacy—and he knew sometimes it was better to ride out a storm rather than trying to beat it back. Something warm and satisfying expanded inside him, knowing she was an arm's length away, her body moving in unison with his. She looked over once and he met her gaze. Her chocolatey eyes glittered at him with devilment. She flashed a challenge of a smile and gave Calico a little nudge to ease her a nose ahead.

He let her take the lead. This time. Because she seemed to need it.

When the horses began to get winded, Meg slowed, bringing them back to a walk. He caught up with her and reined in, the horses' strides matching each other. "Feel better?" he asked mildly.

"Much," she said.

She was actually glowing from the physical exertion, her cheeks with pink roses and her eyes dancing beneath the ugly hat. She looked irresistible, all color and snap.

Clay frowned. Irresistible? Megan? Uh-uh. She was his best friend's little sister. And his friend, too. Meg had always seemed to be able to read him better than anyone. They had known each other so long that defining their relationship was difficult. One distinction was easy enough, though—platonic. Getting involved with Megan Briggs would be messy—Dawson would have his head. Add in the other baggage she brought to the table and he was ready to ride in the other direction—fast. He quickly dismissed the thought.

"I don't think it was just the horses who needed to get out," he observed. "You're wound tighter than a spring. I used to be able to read you like a book. Not anymore. There's too much going on in your head, isn't there?"

"I suppose so. Sometimes I don't know what I'm feeling or thinking. And I'm not good at sitting and waiting."

"Never have been." He chuckled. "Ever."

"Which is probably why I'm feeling so frustrated. I need to *do* something, Clay."

Something seemed to be pulling them together. She trusted him, he realized with surprise. She was confiding in him and he was shocked and a little bit honored considering how they'd left things all those months ago. She'd come to him to share her plans and he'd reacted like everyone else—he hadn't even given her the courtesy of listening.

He could listen now—it wasn't much to ask. He hadn't exactly been supportive up till now. And he'd be honest with her. She would hate for him to be anything else.

"Then tell me your plans," he said as his mare blew out a grand breath and shook her mane, making the bridle hardware jingle.

"You'll think I'm crazy."

"So what? I've thought that for years."

She threw him a "ha-ha, very funny" look and gave Calico's neck a rub. "Part of the reason I went away for my treatment was so that I wouldn't be a burden to anyone. You know that, right? This place has always provided for us, but we've all had to work, even more so since Dad's back went. It was bad enough losing me from the work force when we were already running short. But the added load of caring for me, driving me back and forth to Calgary for treatment, the worry...Mom has enough of that with Dad's appointments. I couldn't ask her to take that on. She's already had to take a job to help with the household expenses, and she somehow juggles everything else, too."

He hadn't realized Linda's job was to bring in much needed income. She'd laughed it away when she started working at Papa's Pizza, insisting it was the perfect antidote to cabin fever now that the kids were grown. "Surely it was more expensive for you to live in Calgary than drive back and forth."

"I stayed with a friend in Springbank. She gave me a job in exchange for room and board. When I was well enough, I worked. The weeks that were too hard, I took it easy." Meg looked up at him, her expression surprisingly open. "Rodeo girls look after each other," she said simply. "Anna and her family were a godsend. Because of their generosity, none of my treatment arrangements cost Mom and Dad a cent."

Clay sat back in the saddle. She'd taken all that on, and her illness as well. "Meg."

"No, don't. I know what you're going to say. Losing a ranch hand hit us hard enough, Clay. I couldn't drain the family resources more than that. I just found another way."

He felt doubly guilty for all the things he'd said to her

that day, all the things he'd accused her of. "It's that bad for you? But Dawson never let on."

"We're not going bankrupt, don't look so alarmed," she said, looking over the fields that seemed to stretch right to the foot of the Rockies miles away. "But we need something more to take us from scraping by to breathing easily."

Clay nodded. "Lots of farmers facing the same choices. What do you have in mind? Alternative stock? Some ranchers I know are turning to sheep."

Meg laughed. "Sheep are so not my thing. Cute and all but no. And no alpacas, either," she added with a smile. "No, what I want is something all my own. Something I can build and nurture and enjoy." She locked her gaze with his and he felt a weird sense of unity and rightness in her sharing her hopes with him. "I'm an equine girl at heart, you know that. I want to expand the stable so we can board horses, and I want to build an indoor ring so I can give lessons."

Clay blew out a breath. Expanding didn't come cheaply. Or quickly. He measured his words, not wanting to discourage but not wanting to give her false hopes, either. "That's a big undertaking."

"Life's short, Clay. I love this farm and I want to see it succeed. Can't I do that while fulfilling dreams of my own?"

The Chinook arch crept across the sky, coming closer, warming the air by degrees. They sat silently, watching the unique formation, feeling the change in the air for several minutes.

"Whatever you're thinking, just say it, Clay."

He didn't look at her, just sat straight in the saddle and stared ahead. How could he explain what he was feeling in the wake of her words? He was a neighbor.

Their families were friends. It didn't seem right that his heart should clench so painfully when she said things like "Life's short."

"Does that mean you're worried about…" He felt like an utter coward not saying the word. Damn it, he was getting too invested already. He should have stayed home this morning. Out of her business. He certainly had enough of his own to keep him occupied.

"Reoccurrence?"

She said the word so plainly it jarred him and he nodded, the brim of his black hat bobbing up and down, his lips set in a grim line.

"I'd be a liar if I said it doesn't cross my mind. But it is not how I choose to live—waiting. Maybe that's why this is so important to me. Life is happening now, and I don't want to miss it."

It had been difficult hearing the news the first time, but even worse now, having eyes wide-open to the possibility that she might go through this again and maybe she wouldn't win the second time around. He'd watched his father battle lung cancer, watched him in daily pain until the end, and he was pretty sure he couldn't go through something like that again with someone he cared about.

Then he thought about his mother, and how she'd walked out on both of them, leaving Aunt Stacy to pick up the slack. Mom had been afraid, too, but she'd run away rather than staying and fighting. For weeks, a young and trusting Clay had been certain that if he wished hard enough, believed long enough, it would all be okay. His mother would come home and his dad would be well again.

When Meg had broken the news of her illness he'd automatically been thrown back to that horrible time. It had brought back so many feelings he'd tried to forget.

He had accused her of running rather than realizing the truth—that she was trying to protect those she loved.

But he didn't need protecting, and there was no *them*. There was just a family friend looking at him right now, asking for advice, giving him a level of respect he wasn't sure he deserved.

"Clay, you and Stacy kept the Gregory place going all these years. You played hard but you worked hard, too, and you're the best rancher I know. You have always been brutally honest with me."

He felt his cheeks heat. He didn't miss the "brutally" part and he knew he'd been too hard on her at times.

"You're the one person I can trust to give me an honest opinion. So what do you think? Can I pull it off?" She looked at him hopefully.

Clay shrugged, not wanting to burst her bubble but needing to impress upon her the challenges she'd face. "The work? You could handle that in your sleep," he said confidently. "I have no doubts about that. But there's more to it. Who will your clients be? Will there be enough to make the business self-sustaining? How will you pay for the expansion?" He paused before he dropped what he knew would feel like an anvil on Megan's hopes. "What happens if you get sick again? Who'll run it? Keep it paying for itself?"

He saw her swallow and she turned her head away. "I *am* crazy then."

"Not crazy." He reached over and grabbed her arm through her heavy coat. "I didn't say it was a bad idea, or impossible. There's a lot of sense in it. It's just not an easy idea and there are things to think about before you move ahead."

Meg's shoulders slumped as she turned her horse toward home. He was an idiot. He should have at least expressed some excitement or said something positive before raining on her parade. "At least you listened," she said darkly as they trudged along. "Mom and Dad wouldn't hear any of it."

"They're just afraid. They've only just got you back."

"They're trying to put me in a bubble."

"They love you and don't want to lose you. So try again. I've never known you to quit anything you really wanted."

"For what it's worth, I was thinking that there'd be plenty of business from the new developments going in. Professional families whose kids want to take lessons. Ask daddy for a pony. You know how it is."

He smiled to himself. Good, she wasn't giving up. "You could be right."

They went along for a few more minutes. The wind was really starting to blow now, stirring up flecks of snow and dirt. Meg turned up the collar of her coat.

"It's the money," she finally said into the awkward silence. "That's why I haven't pushed the issue. I haven't got that kind of capital, obviously. I'll have to go to the bank for it. And the debt is what keeps stopping me up. Mom and Dad can't carry the load." She sighed. "I told you it was foolish."

"Keep thinking about it. You'll come up with a way," he encouraged. "Meg, for God's sake, you beat your illness. You can do anything you set your mind to. Maybe you just need to think outside the box."

The horses sensed the barn was near and picked up their pace a little.

"You were a big help," she acknowledged. "Like I said, no one else would even listen."

"That's what friends do." Friends, he reminded himself. That was the only reason he was feeling so protective of her. So anxious. In Larch Valley friends looked after each other.

Except they didn't always, Clay thought. He certainly hadn't listened to her last year when she'd needed him so very badly. He had closed his heart and his mind to their friendship and "would you believe me if I said I was sorry" didn't quite cut it as far as apologies went.

As they entered the yard, they noticed that both Meg's car and the farm truck were parked next to the house. "Mom and Dad are back from the doctor." She smiled up at Clay. "He saw a specialist about an operation that will help his back and ease the constant pain. Dawson's home, too. You might as well come in and have some cake and talk about whatever it is you really came to talk about."

They turned out the horses in silence and walked up to the house together. Inside the warm kitchen, Linda cut slabs of coffee cake and there was conversation and laughter around the table, just like old times. Meg reached for a mug on a high shelf and Clay found his gaze locked on her breasts. All Dawson had told him was that she'd had surgery, but Clay didn't know to what extent. The curve seemed natural enough, and as her heels touched the floor again he quickly turned his eyes toward the plate of cake in the middle of the table.

She poured the coffee and put cream and sugar next to his mug. He'd been close to the Briggs's for so long she even knew what he took in his coffee. And yet through it all he realized he missed the old camaraderie that used to be between them in years past. The easy friendship was gone but something new, something bigger was taking its place.

Something that made his heart catch. Something he

didn't want to even think about. He never wanted to put himself in a position to be left like his father was. And with Meg, the odds were all against him.

CHAPTER THREE

MEGAN twisted her scarf skillfully around her neck and
adjusted the cap on her head, a funky black knitted item
with a tiny peak at the front. She'd made herself come
into town today, but she'd held back from going hatless.
After seeing Clay's reaction to her short hair she wasn't
quite ready to face a town full of curious neighbors. The
way Mark Squires, the local bank manager, had looked at
her when she'd taken off her cap had told her she'd made
the right call. He'd been completely polite, but she didn't
miss how his gaze had fixed on her hair before travel-
ing down to her face. His eyes had been understanding
and kind, but she knew their meeting began with an automatic subtext, and it had all gone downhill from there.

There would be no loan for the expansion. Meg put her
hand in her coat pocket and ran her fingers over the rock
inside. It had been a silly notion, thinking to rely on her
old good luck charm. And yet she couldn't bring herself
to toss it away. It was just a rock, a piece of brown stone
with an unusual golden streak running down the middle.
But Clay had given it to her when they were just kids.

He'd been angry in those days not long after his father
had died and Stacy had come to live with him. Megan remembered it all quite clearly. "That's very pretty," she'd
commented as he'd turned the rock over in his hands.

Without a smile he'd handed it over. "Then it's yours, Squirt," he'd said, and she'd ignored the horrible nickname simply because Clay had given her something—even if it was just an ordinary rock.

Today she'd dug it out of the box on her dresser and tucked it in her jacket. It seemed fitting that she have a talisman from the one person to be supportive of her dream. He'd been honest but he'd also encouraged her to keep at it and she'd clung to those words. Because of them she'd set up the meeting. It had been for naught but at least she'd tried. Now all she really wanted was a strong coffee and something sinfully chocolatey.

The smells coming from Snickerdoodles bakery were too good to resist. She paused for a moment, wondering if she were up to coming face-to-face with Jen Laramie today. Clay was right about one thing—she'd been avoiding her friends since her return. It didn't matter how many times she practiced lines in her head, she was never quite sure what she would say. She knew she was being a coward and she took a breath and dropped her shoulders. Perhaps with a glass counter between them it would be easier, less personal, a way to break the ice.

She set her lips and put her hand on the doorknob. The bell above the door gave a happy jangle as she stepped inside the shop and its gorgeous blend of scents—brewing coffee, rich chocolate and spicy cinnamon.

A young woman she didn't recognize was behind the counter, and Meg found that despite her resolve she was relieved she wouldn't have to face Jen. She would have to face her friends eventually—she couldn't avoid them forever. Nevertheless, she was still thankful that today wasn't the day, especially when she was so very disappointed at the morning's outcome.

She ordered a gooey, thickly frosted hazelnut brownie

and a large dark roast coffee to go. Meg took her waxed paper packet and coffee cup and made her way outside again into the March sun. She sat on a nearby wooden bench and slid the brownie partly out of the wrapper. The first bite was heaven. The second, fortifying. She took a sip of the strong coffee and sighed. As comfort food went, it didn't quite match up to her mother's beef stew and fresh bread, but for right now it worked. Mark Squires had delivered the bad news and it was either buck up with a jolt of caffeine and cocoa, or wallow in self-pity about yet another thing that cancer had stolen from her. She'd rather work off the calories in the barn than waste precious time feeling sorry for herself.

"Well, well. A public appearance."

Her head snapped up and she nearly bobbled her brownie as Clay's deep voice slid over her nerve endings. Her tongue seemed to tangle in her mouth as she swallowed. She had put her crush behind her, so why in the world did she still find him so gorgeous? It was ridiculous that a rush of heat flew into her cheeks and her hands grew slippery at the mere sound of his voice.

Today he wore a black Stetson and a brown ranch jacket above jeans and boots. His mouth turned up in one corner while his eyes twinkled at her, taking the sting out of the words, leaving her completely at his mercy. She remembered the way his gaze had followed her the last time he'd been at her house. She'd avoided eye contact, but she'd been completely aware of the way his eyes had zeroed in on her rather than focusing on his cake.

She sighed and cut herself some slack. She was a woman after all. And Clay Gregory had that effect on just about every female in Larch Valley, including those with bifocals and old enough to be his grandmother. She reminded herself that he also knew exactly how charming he could be. It went a long way toward cooling her jets.

She took a deliberate sip of coffee. "I'm not a total hermit, you know."

He chuckled. "I'm glad to hear it. And sitting on a bench in the sunshine no less. What's the occasion?"

She considered for a moment and then wondered what she had to lose by being truthful. "Drowning my sorrows."

The half smile evaporated. "Are you feeling okay?"

Meg fought back irritation. This is how it would always be. Something would go wrong and everyone would automatically assume it was her health.

"I'm fine."

When she didn't elaborate Clay shifted his weight and looked pointedly at the seat beside her. "May I?"

The fact that he asked rather than simply took it upon himself to sit down made something warm curl inside Meg's stomach. For all her feminine reactions, they *were* friends. Or at least they used to be. She slid the brownie back inside the wrapper and nodded. "Of course."

His large form seemed to dwarf the wood and iron bench and Meg swallowed. When she met his gaze, his chocolate eyes held concern. Maybe things weren't as over for her as she'd thought. Being next to Clay, having his undivided attention, brought all sorts of old feelings to the surface. Feelings that would be better if they remained buried, all things considered.

"Anything I can do?"

Of all the things she expected him to say, the simple offer had been furthest from her mind. "Not really," she answered. This was her problem, and it was up to her to find a solution—if there was one. "Looks like my big plan is a bust after all."

His brow pulled together in the way she knew it would. "What do you mean, it's a bust?"

"I met with the bank today. I can't get a loan, and no loan, no expansion. Simple."

Only three days ago she had been on horseback, looking down over the ranch and sharing her plans with Clay. She'd been able to see it all in her head—the new building with the riding ring, the horses grazing in the pasture, the corral where she taught youngsters how to ride and put their mounts through their paces.

Now it was all gone in a puff of smoke, and she felt foolish for telling him anything. She hated failure, but in particular she hated failing in Clay's eyes. Clay had always done every single thing he'd put his mind to. Nothing had ever stood in his way, no matter how much adversity he'd faced, and he'd had his share.

"I'm sorry, Meg. Maybe there's a way you can get the bank to reconsider."

She shook her head and tossed her coffee cup in the garbage can next to her bench. The flavor had suddenly gone stale and flat. "I don't see how. I have no collateral to back me up. The only way is to get Mom and Dad to cosign and I refuse to let them take on the burden of this project. I won't put the ranch at risk. They've just paid off the mortgage and they're still just scraping by."

Clay remained silent, which only served to cement the facts in Meg's mind. "Even if I did get financing, I would have a hard time insuring the loan," she continued, the final nail in the coffin. "With my medical history…"

Clay put his hand on her knee, a gesture she was sure was meant to be reassuring, but his touch seemed to burn through her trousers right through to her skin. She bit down on her lip.

"Don't give up yet, Meg. When life puts up a road-block, you have three choices."

"I do?" She lifted her head and met his gaze. The half smile was back and he patted her knee before removing his hand.

"You can give up, you can bust through it, or you can go around it."

"I don't want to give up."

"Then don't. It might take some time, but a way will come. You'll see."

But she didn't want to take her time. Time was too precious these days and she was hungry for everything. How could she explain that to him? She couldn't, not without going into details about the last year. Details she wasn't comfortable sharing and ones that she knew Clay wouldn't be comfortable hearing. There was nothing like staring death in the eye to prompt a sense of urgency to live in the present.

"I hope you're right."

"Of course I am. You're not a quitter, Meg." He nudged her arm. "So you stopped for a chocolate fix?"

"I shouldn't have. Lord knows it doesn't solve any-thing." She brushed off his question but couldn't help the tiny ray of hope that still glimmered. Clay didn't have a solution, but he wasn't simply nodding his head and say-ing sorry she'd failed. He believed in her, and he had no idea how much that meant at this moment.

He laughed. "I've lived with a woman long enough to know that chocolate brownies can cure a lot of ills."

Meg smiled. His aunt Stacy. The woman had stepped in when Clay had been a boy and raised him as her own. Now she was getting a second chance at love and Meg thought it was lovely. "Well, maybe." She nudged his elbow back. "But eventually the brownie's gone and reality is still there, staring you in the face."

"Reality is, you only fail if you quit. So don't quit."

She turned her head to study his face. It was utterly relaxed, showing a confidence in her that she didn't necessarily feel in herself. She might have confusing feelings where Clay was concerned, but today she was glad he'd stopped. She'd needed the dose of no-nonsense optimism.

"Thanks," she said quietly. "For the pep talk."

He raised an eyebrow. "Lots of people will get behind you, you'll see. Speaking of, did you see Jen inside?"

"No. She wasn't in."

"She's not in the bakery as often these days, I hear." He nodded at a neighbor passing by, then rested his elbows on his knees. "Andrew says he wishes she'd take it easier now that there's a baby on the way. She has catering jobs booked right up until her due date he says. Stacy's wedding is one of them."

"When's Stacy's big day?"

Clay crossed an ankle over his knee. Lord, where did he get the energy? He couldn't seem to sit still and it made Meg smile.

"Three weeks. The second Saturday in April. She's practically moved everything to Pincher Creek already."

Meg knew Stacy Gregory had reconnected with her high-school sweetheart and they were finally making a go of it. "It seems odd thinking of your place without her," she said. For years it had been the two of them running the Gregory ranch. The thought of Clay alone in the rambling house left an empty feeling in Meg's heart.

"I won't deny I'm going to miss her," he admitted. "She's all the family I've got. But I'm a big boy," he replied with a low laugh. "I can take care of myself."

"Of course you can!" Meg felt flustered beneath the warmth of his steady gaze. "I never meant to imply otherwise."

"As long as you don't start acting like Stacy. She's been hovering and cooking and freezing things for weeks, like I'm going to starve if she's not there." He rolled his eyes. "I don't know why she has to flutter so much. We've shared the cooking before. I can manage to not poison myself."

At his disgruntled expression Megan felt her remaining jitters melt away. "It might not have anything to do with you. Maybe she's nervous, Clay, and needs something to keep her hands busy."

He pondered for a moment. "No, I think it's more than that. She's been pushing me to bring a date to the wedding. I'm telling you, Meg, weddings make women stir-crazy. All of a sudden they think everyone in the universe should be paired up."

The air had warmed since the recent cold snap and Meg loved the feel of the early spring sun on her face. It was good to chat about a different topic, putting the focus on someone else and such a happy occasion. "Weddings are a big deal," she answered, and at Clay's raised brow, she amended, "So I've heard."

"I don't know why she thinks I need a date."

"Someone to pin on your boutonniere?"

"My what?"

Meg really laughed this time. Putting Clay on the back foot was much more fun than thinking about everything that had gone wrong this morning. As distractions went, he was fairly helpful, and for the first time since coming home she felt a return to the easy friendship they'd enjoyed years past. She let her eyes sparkle at him. "See?

That's why. Your flower, silly, on your lapel. I'm assuming you're in the wedding party."

"I'm giving her away. Then it's just a dinner, right?"

"And a dance, so Mom said."

"Well, whatever. Just because she's getting married she thinks she can match me up. She suggested Tara Stillwell as if she didn't already know Dawson's staked his claim there."

Meg's head whipped around. How had things become that serious so quickly? There were times she still felt so out of the loop while Clay seemed to know everything. "Staked his claim? She's not a parcel of land, Clay."

"You know what I mean. There are rules and I'm no poacher. Besides, I'm not interested in Tara, for all she's a nice girl."

"Are you interested in anyone?" she asked—and then held her breath waiting for an answer.

What had made her ask? Why did it matter if he had his eye on a girl? Why shouldn't he? It shouldn't bother her in the least. But it did. She didn't want him for herself anymore but the thought of him *being* with someone…it felt wrong.

"No. When I said that she said I should ask Lisa Hamm or Emily Dodds—you know, Agnes's granddaughter? It was all I could do to put her off. There's a dance, she said." He took off his hat and ran his hand over his thick, dark hair, clearly agitated. "If I'm not with someone it'll be open season, she said. Which is ridiculous."

It wasn't ridiculous at all. If Clay went unattached, there'd be a dozen pair of hungry eyes waiting to be asked to dance—or doing the asking themselves. It was nice to know Clay's ego wasn't so inflated that he realized it.

That wouldn't be a concern for Meg. If she went—and she hadn't decided if she would or not—she'd be holding up a wall somewhere. Who would ask her to dance? She grimaced. She'd be a curiosity. Lots of people looking but keeping her at arm's length. On one hand, it was what she wanted, because physical contact still made her nervous. But on the other it was damned awkward in a social situation. Which was exactly why she'd avoided those thus far.

"You're a pretty eligible guy, Clay." Meg turned on the bench so she faced him better. "You're not exactly hard to look at. You're in your prime with a lovely ranch all to yourself. Where Larch Valley's concerned, you're prime marriage material."

Clay looked so horrified Meg nearly choked on the laughter that bubbled up. "Shut up!" he said, putting his hat more firmly on his head. "That's not true."

"Oh, it so is," she answered, having fun now. Clay had done his share of teasing over the years and it was gratifying to put the shoe on the other foot. "Add in the fact that you'll be all spic-and-span in a suit and they won't be able to resist. They'll be falling all over you, wanting to dance. To catch your eye. Maybe something else." She waggled her eyebrows for effect. "And then there's the throwing of the bouquet and the tossing of the garter…"

"Megan!" He said it loudly enough that a passerby turned to stare before carrying on down Main Avenue. He lowered his voice. "I know you're teasing but that's not funny. I'm not interested. Not in anyone. Definitely not in marriage."

Once more that odd little hole of emptiness threatened to widen. The bitterness she'd always sensed in him where marriage was concerned hadn't mellowed over the years. Not that she could blame him. How did one get over being abandoned by their one remaining parent? Times had been rough for the Gregory family, but Clay's mom hadn't toughed it out. For better or worse, sickness and health…that hadn't mattered. They'd never really talked about it, but Megan could understand at least that much. Clay hadn't had the strong example of a good marriage that she'd had growing up.

"All I'm saying is that Stacy is on to something. If you went with a date, you'd save yourself a lot of trouble. You just have to find someone with no romantic aspirations."

"Who are you going with?"

Her gaze flitted away. "I've been included in the family invitation," she said quietly. She hadn't even decided yet if she was going. She didn't know what to wear, knew nothing in her closet suited the changes to her figure. She had barely even shown her face around town, let alone show up at the first big social event of the spring. And it would be a big event. Weddings in the valley always were. At least when she'd first thought about it, she'd pictured being able to share news of how she was picking up and carrying on with her own business. Proof that she was fine and standing on her own two feet. Now she had none of that to bolster her. Poor, pathetic Megan, back on the family ranch, showing up with her parents. Ugh!

"Go with me."

Her heart took a leap before settling back down. "I don't need a pity invitation," she whispered, swallowing around the thick lump that had suddenly appeared in her throat. How had the balance of the conversation shifted so quickly and completely? She'd enjoyed having the upper hand and now here she was, feeling at a disadvantage again.

"Pity? It's me that needs the pity." His gaze was utterly earnest. "You're the perfect date. Anyone else would get ideas, like you said. There's never been any of that between you and me."

Clearly he had no clue of her earlier crush and it was just as well it stayed that way. Meg blinked. Could Clay really be so blind that he'd never sensed how she'd felt? She nearly blushed just thinking about it. She'd never been the kind of girl to try to stand out, but she'd always hoped he'd notice.

But that was before. She'd grown up a lot over the last few years—first when her father had been injured and couldn't work the ranch anymore, and then with her illness. There were no such things as fairy tales and wishes. There was hard work and determination and practicalities. Reality had a way of hitting and keeping one's head out of the clouds. And right now Clay was suggesting she go to a wedding as his date—not because he wanted a date but because she was a safe bet. She was protection.

She was a practical girl, but the complete absence of any sort of romance cut her. Was she so undesirable then? She'd always liked being "one of the boys" when it came to the ranch work. But that had been before, when she'd been confident, and, well, *whole*. She hadn't cared as much then. "I'm sorry, Clay, I haven't even decided if I'm going or not."

"Not go? But Aunt Stacy will be so disappointed. Your mom is standing up with her, you know. Your whole family is going. Of course you'll be there."

"Like I said, I haven't decided."

He pressed his back into the bench slats and stretched out his legs, crossing them at the ankle. "How will it look if you don't go?"

"I'm sure Stacy will understand."

"I don't mean Stacy. What do you think everyone else will think? You're home from the hospital but you're hardly seen out of the house. Everyone will wonder if you're really fine. Rumors will get started."

Her temper started to simmer. "I didn't realize you had your ear so close to the grapevine," she said tightly. "Your concern is very touching."

Clay's eyes sparked. "You were the one who said you wanted everyone to think you were strong and fit. Isn't that why you went away in the first place? So no one would see you at the worst? What does it say now that you're home and you're hiding away?"

She hated that he was right. She hated that he was insightful enough to anticipate that her absence would cause more speculation than her presence and yet could be so blind to other things. And she hated that he knew her well enough to use it.

"Maybe that I want some privacy."

Clay let out a derisive snort. "Privacy? In Larch Valley? Come on, Meg. You know better than that. People are always going to talk."

She grabbed on to the straw he offered. "That's right. And if I go with you, what do you think they'll say?"

She had him there, and he paused for a moment. "So what? We'll know the truth. And if we go together it means neither of us will have to go through the day alone. You'll have my back and I'll have yours. Just like it's always been."

The retort that sat on Meg's lips died. It was true—the idea of going through the day alone was a major issue. Her mom and dad would be together. Dawson would be with Tara. Megan would be on her own, the odd woman out. Conspicuous. Fair game for curious minds and any number of well-intentioned but sympathetic questions. Wasn't that the real reason she'd stayed close to home since her return? Even now, sitting on the bench, she was aware of curious gazes in her direction. It was only Clay's presence that kept them at a distance. She didn't want to hide behind him, but she couldn't deny that the idea of facing the day together was much better than walking into a room alone.

"I don't need your protection," she replied, but she was weakening. He was right. Again. It annoyed her but it couldn't be disputed. With Clay on her arm perhaps the partygoers would have something else to talk about.

"And I don't need yours, either. Both of us could make it through the evening on our own. Hell, I planned to and told Stacy as much. You have to admit, though, it makes sense. Come on, Meg." He smiled and her heart gave a little lurch. "You won't subject me to the likes of Lisa Hamm, will you?"

"Lisa's a nice girl."

She certainly was, but she and Clay would never suit. Lisa was high maintenance, high-strung and a bit needy. Meg could never see her as a rancher's wife. Clay needed someone easier. Someone low-key, easygoing. Someone to work beside him, a partner and not a pet.

"She's not my type and you know it, Megan Briggs."

Her lips twitched at the thought of Clay choking on a tie while Lisa and her five-inch heels flitted about him.

"I haven't been a very good friend lately, and I know it. I really am sorry for what I said last spring. Can't we go back to how it used to be?"

In a way how it used to be sounded great, but she also realized it wasn't enough anymore. Not for her. But he was offering an olive branch and it would be petty not to accept it. In the end she couldn't refuse, not when he looked at her in the warm, conspiratorial way he was looking at her right now.

"All right. We'll go together."

"Awesome." He sat up and clapped his hands on his knees. "There's one problem solved. That's the trick,

Meg. Finding solutions that benefit both parties. You help me, I help you. Everyone goes home happy."

He had no idea.

"I'll see you around, Squirt." He got up from the bench and shook out his pant legs while Meg sat, feeling like she'd been hit broadside and left completely off balance. How had this all happened in the space of an hour?

She looked down at her wax paper bag. The hazelnut brownie was a mangled, gooey mess inside.

"Yeah, see you," she mumbled, avoiding his gaze and reaching for her purse and keys.

"Megan."

She looked up at him, not wanting him to know how flustered she suddenly felt, and how childish and small he'd made her feel by employing her old nickname.

"About your project…don't give up. You'll find a way. You always do."

To her surprise he lifted a finger to the brim of his hat before walking away. For all his faults and little annoyances, she'd just been reminded that Clay Gregory was a gentleman. And that she, as a woman, wasn't impervious to his charms.

They had a date. To a wedding. A wedding where she'd have to wear heels and a dress and fix her hair…

She put her fingers to her lips as the panic set in. What on earth had she just gotten herself into?

CHAPTER FOUR

It HAD taken Meg a week to gather up the courage to visit Lily's boutique, and she'd played with the idea of going to Calgary and being another anonymous customer in some chain store. But she knew Clay was right about some things—one being that she couldn't avoid people forever. Between Lily's own unique designs and her carefully selected stock, she'd surely have something to suit Meg's needs. It was time Meg stopped being afraid. And the wedding date was growing closer. In a way, she was grateful for the push the shopping trip provided.

It didn't stop the nerves from jumping around in her tummy, though. When she entered the store, Lily was helping another customer and didn't see her come in. Meg browsed while waiting, but every single dress that didn't belong on her mother—or grandmother—was either sleeveless or had a much too revealing neckline.

Meg dropped her hand from the dress rack and sighed. She had nerves of steel while waiting for the start of a race but the simple task of choosing a dress for Stacy's wedding had her in a tizzy. It wasn't just the need to be girly. It was the added challenge of finding something she was comfortable in, considering the fact that she was still wearing supportive bras with a breast form tucked inside. She held out a misty-blue strapless concoction.

How could she possibly conceal the extent of her surgery in something like this?

Maybe she should just tell Clay she couldn't go.

But that would be chickening out, and as nervous as she was, she didn't want to be called a coward. She moved to the next rack. There had to be something here in Lily's shop that would suit. And if she had to ask for help, she would. She kept hearing Clay's rich voice calling her Squirt. She wasn't that girl any longer. She was a woman. She'd been through trials and come out stronger and by God, she'd show him that.

Which sounded fine and grand, except for the quivering in her stomach that said she was still unsure about how to explain her particular problem to Lily.

"Megan?"

The bubble of nervousness popped as Meg heard her name. She looked up to see Lily coming toward her wearing a wide smile. Meg was instantly aware of the difference in their appearances. She wore neat jeans and a cotton shirt, while Lily was dressed in classic stovepipe trousers and a ruffled blouse that suited her perfectly. It didn't happen often, but at times she was envious of the innate style Lily possessed. When Lily had quit her job as a home economics teacher and opened her shop, no one had been surprised. She had a certain knack for designing and Meg knew Lily's business was gaining notice in larger cities.

"Lily." Meg started to smile back but before she could compose herself Lily had folded her into a tight hug and Meg felt the beginnings of panic.

Thankfully Lily's embrace was brief and she stepped back. Meg collected herself as best she could, folding her arms in front of her and pasting on a smile. This was her dear friend, the woman who'd come to Larch Valley and fit in as though she'd lived here all her life. When a baby was born there was a hand-quilted crib set from Lily. If someone was sick, a casserole showed up, accompanied by a helping hand around the house. Lily was the most generous, kind woman Meg had ever known. The hug was a matter of course. But Meg was still so very self-conscious.

"We've been wondering when you were going to turn up," Lily smiled. "Drew said he saw you outside the bakery with Clay the other day. Oh, I'm so glad you've come in. We missed you."

The welcome was warm but Meg heard Clay's voice in her head. Larch Valley was small and people were going to talk, no matter what. It was the blessing and curse of a small town. There was always a core of caring and concern, but everyone knew your business, too. Even an innocent conversation over a brownie was of note and spread through circles of friends.

"I'm looking for a dress," Meg blurted, hugely uncomfortable now and unsure how to proceed. Perhaps she wouldn't have felt so very awkward if she had made an effort to reconnect as soon as she'd come back to town. She looked up at Lily for help. "I'm going to Stacy's wedding and I don't have anything to wear."

Lily's face blanked with confusion at Meg's less than personal greeting and Meg cringed inside. She hadn't meant to sound so brusque. Lily was a close friend, not some clerk.

Lily's face cleared and she carried on smoothly. "This would be lovely with your coloring." She held up the ice-blue dress that Meg had held in her hands just moments before. "Your hair's come in lighter than before, with those gorgeous coppery highlights. With your creamy complexion it'd be perfect."

Lily's matter-of-fact remark startled Meg and she touched the tips of her hair self-consciously. "It's not very feminine," she said quietly. "Don't you think that dress is a bit…frilly next to my hairstyle?"

Lily shook her head. "Nonsense, Meg. It's come in soft and gorgeous. If anything you look exotic and stylish."

Meg felt gratitude fill her heart. Lily wasn't just generous, she was genuine. She'd overlooked Meg's stilted responses and Meg loved her for it. "Thank you, Lil," she replied, relaxing a little. "It takes some getting used to."

"I think you should leave it that way. Now, what about the dress?" She shook the hanger in her hands, making the fabric shimmer.

"It's lovely, but I'm not sure strapless is my thing. I was hoping for something a little more…subdued."

Lily's eyebrows puckered in the middle. "Hmm. We might need some help," she mused. "Hold this." She shoved a dress into Meg's hands and headed straight to the door.

"Where are you going?" Meg called after her.

"Reinforcements!" Lily called back. Thirty seconds later she was back with Jen in tow.

"Never fear! The fashion police are here!"

Jen rushed down the aisle to greet Meg while Lily locked up the store behind her. Meg felt her heart contract. Jen wasn't showing much, but her tummy was slightly bubbled out in pregnancy and her skin glowed. Meg loved her friends but felt at an immediate disadvantage. They were so beautiful, secure in their marriages, planning families. Meg had none of those things. She felt like a complete ugly duckling.

Worse, she felt the stirrings of jealousy. She knew it was completely unfair of her. There had been no question of doing chemo and radiation. They'd been necessary to keep her alive. But looking at Jen, expecting a baby and so utterly happy…Meg was fully aware of all the side effects of cancer treatment, immediate and down the road. Even if she could conceive, it could be very, very difficult. Another river for her to cross.

Jen gave Meg a quick hug and Meg pushed her melancholy thoughts aside. She would not begrudge Jen an iota of happiness. It wasn't her fault. It wasn't anyone's fault. It was just the way things were.

"What are you two up to?" Meg looked from Jen to Lily and back again.

"I'm closing up so we can find you the perfect dress."

"But…but…"

Jen looked at Lily. "She's lost some weight. My dresses won't fit her, even if I'm not using them at the moment." She put her hand on her swelling tummy. "Yours might."

Lily shook her head. "No, I'm too hippy. Besides, Meg deserves something new, don't you think?"

Meg felt completely bulldozed and slightly invisible. This hadn't been part of the plan! While it was wonderful to see her friends and to know that they hadn't changed over the past months, she knew they had a tendency to get carried away and Meg didn't want to get carried right with them. "Hello, I'm right here."

"Of course you are, isn't this fun?"

Shopping for dresses was not what Meg normally classified as fun. She had never had much for hips and now her curves above the waist were…well, under renovation was probably the politest way she could explain it. "I appreciate it, you two, but really. A simple dress for Stacy's wedding is all I need," she insisted. "Nothing over the top."

"Honey." Jen and Lily each took one of her hands. Jen's eyes suddenly welled up with unshed tears. "You wouldn't let us do anything for you when you got sick. As stubborn, independent women ourselves, we understood it and accepted it. But please, Meg. Let us help you now. We're so glad you're home. It's so good to have the three of us together again. If only Lucy were here, it would be like old times."

The tears threatened to spill over. "After what you've been through, don't you think you deserve this?" Jen asked.

Meg was incredibly touched and her earlier thoughts evaporated. She was so blessed to have friends like Jen and Lily, and yet she was scared to open herself up too much. She wasn't used to voluntarily making herself vulnerable, but they had to understand that this couldn't be just any dress. Not for her figure. She swallowed, knowing inside that she could trust them both. She had never had sisters, but Jen and Lily were about as close as she'd ever come. "It's not just the dress," she whispered, pulling her hands away. "It's the style I'm worried about. You see I…"

She couldn't form the next words.

It was Lily who clued in first. "Oh, Meg. It's the mastectomy, isn't it?"

She nodded as relief flooded her—it was good to finally get it out in the open. Lily's husband, Noah, had lost an arm in Afghanistan. By the time they'd married he'd gotten his prosthetic, but Meg remembered clearly how difficult Noah had found the adjustment. It was natural that Lily was the one to put the pieces together.

"I haven't done reconstruction. Right now I'm wearing a form on that side, and my bras are…well, they're not exactly the frilly, pretty sort."

"Shoot, we can get you a new bra." Jen smiled.

"It's not just that," Meg protested, handing Lily the

garment in her hands. "It's a comfort thing. I'm…it's…" Meg looked up helplessly. She hadn't told a living soul how she felt about how she looked now. Not even in the support group she'd attended in Calgary.

"What is it?" Jen put her arm around Meg's shoulders. "You're safe here, Meg. We consider you family and we love you."

Meg's lip began to wobble as her face crumpled. All her defenses disintegrated at the heartfelt words. "Oh," she wailed, "you weren't supposed to say that!"

She couldn't stop the tears that came. Lily went to the back and brought out a chair and she sank into it, covering her face with her hands. What was wrong with her? It wasn't dress shopping that was stressing her out. It was looking at her scars, day in and day out. Seeing one "normal" side and the other ravaged by the surgeon's knife. Now she was supposed to go to this wedding—with Clay!—and the last thing she felt was pretty and feminine.

She finally caught her breath and blew her nose into the tissue Jen offered. She had needed to do that for a long time. Tears were something she hadn't indulged in during her treatment and it seemed now that the worst was over those emotions were coming out bit by bit. She'd felt fragile for weeks, but now she felt better, less tangled up, more ready to tackle the job ahead. "I'm sorry, you guys. I've felt so self-conscious, so afraid, that I've avoided everyone. I should have come to you before."

"You came when you were ready," Jen answered simply, squatting down next to Meg's chair and putting a hand on her knee. "It's okay. You've been through a lot. Just remember we've always got your back."

Those were the exact words Clay had used and Meg's pulse gave a little kick. "I feel ugly," she admitted. "My hair is like a boy's and so is…" She swallowed. "Let's just say my bikini days are long gone."

"You are so not ugly. The shorter hair makes your eyes pop and highlights your cheekbones. And honestly—no one can tell about the other."

"I used to be comfortable in my own skin."

Lily nodded thoughtfully. "Yes, that's a problem. It's hard to be sexy when you don't feel sexy."

Meg's lashes snapped up. "Sexy? I never said anything about wanting to be sexy!"

"Every woman wants to feel confident and pretty, Meg. Besides, you're going to want a dance partner aren't you? You can't dance with your daddy all night."

Meg's insides curled with embarrassment. "I'll dance with Drew and Noah and Dawson, too."

Jen sighed. "Meg."

Meg stood up. She didn't want to be pitied or patronized. "Are you saying no one will want to dance with me?"

Jen shrugged and looked away.

Meg lifted her chin. "I'll dance with Clay, after all we're going together."

Her mouth clamped shut as soon as the words were out. Lily and Jen looked at each other and grinned and Meg realized she'd been played—and she'd fallen straight into their trap. They'd wanted to prompt her into a reaction and it had worked. She wished she could take the words back. Now they'd be inventing a romance where there was none.

"So, you're going with Clay," Lily said speculatively.

"Just as friends," Meg tried to explain. "He didn't have a date and neither did I and Stacy put the fear of God in him about being a target for singles."

"Which he definitely is. He's gorgeous." Jen grinned.

"Hey, I still have eyes," she defended when Lily gave her arm a nudge.

Meg remembered a time when Clay and Dawson had rescued Drew and Jen during a snowstorm. Drew had been pretty clear about marking his territory, and he and Jen had been stuck together like glue ever since. Drew didn't have a thing to worry about and they all knew it.

"It's not a date date," she insisted. "For heaven's sake, he still calls me Squirt."

"Would you like it to be? A date date?"

Jen's quiet question threw Meg for a loop. She'd never said a word about her feelings for Clay to anyone. And she'd given up on him ages ago. The flutters she'd gotten lately meant nothing. And yet the idea of knocking his socks off held a certain appeal. What would it be like to feel like a real woman again? Was that even possible?

"Clay doesn't think of me that way," she reiterated.

"That's because he only sees you in jeans and boots," Lily said, casting an appraising glance over Meg's clothing. "Functional for ranch work, but not so great for snaring a man."

"I am not looking to snare anyone!"

"Here she goes, protesting again."

She wasn't taking the bait this time. She knew her work wear was functional, but it also did a fine job of concealing shapes she wanted to conceal. "All teasing aside, you two, I just want a nice, pretty dress that covers what I need to have covered to feel comfortable. As far as Clay Gregory goes, I'm to be his dinner partner and a friend to rescue him from the clutches of Lisa Hamm, apparently."

Jen and Lily both smiled. "I think we've given her a hard enough time, don't you?" Lily asked Jen, nudging her with her elbow. She smiled at Meg. "That'll teach you for giving us the brush-off."

"I never meant…"

"Hush," Lily said kindly. "We're going to find you a beautiful dress, Meg. And if we don't, I'll make you one. I can accomplish a lot in three weeks."

Jen put her arm around Meg's shoulders. "Consider us your fairy godmothers," she added. "Your debut back into Larch Valley society will be a smash hit. I'm thinking red, Lil, how 'bout you?"

For the first time in months, Meg felt the tiniest bit pretty. As her best friends led her to the next rack, she thought about Clay, his saucy smirk, and how gratifying it would be to wipe it off his face. She could do this. She would. It was time she set the tone for the rest of her life and it was time that tone was one of success. Maybe a dress and a wedding didn't sound like much of a start, but she had to begin somewhere.

"I like red," Meg said clearly. She grinned as she imagined the look on Clay's face when she showed up at Stacy's wedding in a knockout dress and heels. He wouldn't be able to accuse her of hiding away then. "What the heck, you guys. In for a penny, in for a pound, eh?"

For the tenth time in as many minutes, Clay fiddled with his bow tie. He'd hoped Stacy would have gone in for a more casual Western wedding, where he could have worn his good boots and a bolo. At least then he might have felt slightly at home in this monkey suit. But no, she'd gone for the whole hog. Black tuxedo, strangling bow tie, shoes so shiny he could see his reflection. The white rose boutonniere was pinned to his lapel courtesy of Meg's mother, who'd been at the house helping the bride get ready. The pianist was playing something soft and classical for the arriving guests. Clay smiled tightly and nodded at a neighbor who had just arrived—in white shirt and bolo tie. "Isn't he lucky," Clay grumbled under his breath.

He was nervous. Mike Schuyler, the groom, seemed more relaxed than Clay was, shaking hands with the minister and preparing to make his way to the front of the church. Clay checked his watch and adjusted the cuffs of his jacket. Stacy was due any second with Linda beside her. He'd caught a glimpse of the bride before he'd headed to the church. Stacy's simple white dress suited her perfectly. It was hard to believe that the woman who'd raised him was getting married. He was thrilled for her. And he liked Mike.

But giving her away was going to be difficult. She was, in all but one sense of the word, his mother. And placing his mother into another man's keeping was a difficult thing to do.

A hand clapped on to his shoulder. "God, you look like you could use a nip of something," Dawson greeted him with a wide smile. "Relax. It's not like you're the one getting hitched."

Clay forced a smile. No, it wasn't him. Thank God. This was torture enough. Standing up at the front of the church? It wasn't likely that would ever happen. "Dawson. And Tara. You look great."

Tara smiled shyly at him and put her arm through Dawson's. "Thanks, Clay."

If Dawson was here then Meg must be, too. Clay hadn't seen her since last week when he'd popped over to the Briggs ranch to talk to Dawson about renting out a block of land for grazing. Meg's words about the Briggs's struggles had stayed with him and the arrangement would benefit both operations. Meg had been talking to the vet, her back to him and that awful ugly hat on her head. Before he left he'd quickly asked, "Are we still on for the wedding?" She'd answered that she'd meet him at the church.

What had he expected? It's not like it was a real date. She was a friend. She was his wingman, right? She was going to help him get through the evening and he'd be by her side as she faced the town again. And at the barn she'd acted like it was nothing to her at all. He frowned a little.

"Did Meg come with you?"

Dawson's grin widened. "She sure did."

"I think she went to the powder room," Tara suggested.

Dawson's grin faded a touch. "I'll admit I was surprised when she said you were going together."

Clay met Dawson's steady gaze. "As friends without other dates. That's all."

Dawson's gaze was unerring. "Good. She needs support, you know? But not complications. Not after what she's been through."

"And you consider me a complication?" Clay was tall but Dawson was a bit taller and right now it annoyed Clay a lot to have to look up at his best friend, especially when Dawson spoke with that hint of warning deepening his voice.

"I'm just saying we all know your history, Clay. Be careful."

"It's just Meg. Nothing to worry about, so you don't need to act all big brother with me."

Dawson frowned. "Well, you haven't seen her yet." He nodded toward the foyer.

Clay turned his head to scan the vestibule.

She was there. Smiling and holding Agnes Dodds's hand between her own and then turning away as they parted.

Holy Mother Mary. The air seemed to leave Clay's lungs as he stared at her. Where was the plain old Meg he remembered? The woman walking this way was stunning. More than stunning. She was...

His brain seemed to tie in knots as she suddenly saw him and stopped. For the space of a heartbeat, their gazes clashed and her lips dropped open the tiniest bit. Full, sexy lips the exact same deep red hue as her dress. She gave a slow smile and his body tightened in response. When had she learned to do that? Why was he reacting this way? Sure, he'd noticed she was attractive but she wasn't his type. She was his best friend's little sister. Only she wasn't, not today. Today he couldn't take his eyes off her. She was soft, sweet and sexy as hell.

She began walking again and Clay had the strangest urge to run, only he wasn't sure if he wanted to run to her or away from her. His gaze swept down to her hips, lightly swaying as she made her way past the gathering congregation to his side. He shouldn't be having these thoughts about Megan. All he wanted right this moment was to put his hands on her slim hips and draw her close.

Dawson's hand gave a final tap on his shoulder but Clay barely registered the touch. She was only a few feet away now and he had to somehow untangle his tongue and be cool.

Meg's whole body felt on fire beneath the heat of Clay's gaze.

At first there'd been a jolt as their eyes met and recognition flared. Then had come the sweetest part—the utter surprise and approval she glimpsed in his face. She felt the glow of triumph as she smiled slowly and his dark eyes glittered at her in response. He stood up straighter.

She saw Dawson say something by Clay's shoulder, but Clay's eyes never left hers.

Today she felt as beautiful as she'd ever been, which under the circumstances felt tantamount to a miracle.

Her confidence faltered slightly as she reached him and struggled to find the right thing to say. She'd seen his reaction to her appearance and she didn't want to blow the moment by sounding stupid. In the end she managed a simple but inadequate sounding "Hi" as she looked up at him, grateful for once to have on heels. At least in her shoes her eyes were at a level with his strong, freshly shaved jaw.

"You look...wow," he finished, at a loss for words, and Meg felt her confidence come rushing back.

"Thanks. Lily made the dress."

"It suits you."

Goose bumps erupted on her bare arms. She'd made noises about not going sleeveless but Lily had worked her magic with a soft wrap-style bodice and a demure V-neck that gathered into wide shoulder straps. The red velvet was soft and rich, and the fabric and construction were very pretty while managing to make Meg feel covered and comfortable. Jen had loaned her gold dangly earrings and a simple gold necklace. Megan couldn't have felt more like a princess had she been the bride.

Clay was staring at her oddly, the silence somewhat awkward but in a new, exciting sort of way. He put a hand lightly on her waist. "I need to go for now, Stacy's arrived."

The spot where his fingers touched seemed to light on fire through the fabric, and she wasn't sure but she thought she detected a bit of regret in his words. "And I need to find my seat." The words came out sort of breathlessly and Meg bit down on her lip. There was knock-

ing his socks off and there was making a fool of herself
and the way she was feeling with his hand on her waist
was treading on fool territory. It felt proprietary—and
she liked it. Too much. She could get used to that feeling
a bit too easily, and she reminded herself that this was
a special day. This was not real life. Tomorrow she'd be
back in faded jeans, out in the barns again.

But, for today, she was determined to put her cares
aside and enjoy every blessed moment.

"I'll see you after?"

His warm eyes looked at her hopefully and she couldn't
stop the smile from forming. "I'm sure you'll have other
duties, like family pictures, that sort of thing. Why don't
I just meet up with you at the reception?"

He looked like he wanted to say something more but
she had to move, had to escape his touch before she did
something silly. She'd achieved what she wanted. She was
making a success of the afternoon, wasn't she? There was
no more to it than that.

With a parting smile she drew away from his hand and
walked toward the sanctuary doors. She swore she could
feel his gaze on her back and she forced herself to take
regular breaths. She wouldn't look back at him. There
was obvious, and then there was *obvious*.

She took her seat beside her father and crossed her
legs, smoothing her skirt. But for a moment she fiddled
with the hem. It had gone far better than she'd dreamed.
There was only one flaw in her plan. Later she was going
to have to dance with Clay. Her skin still tingled where
his hand had rested. If she reacted like this over a simple
touch, what would happen when he held her in his arms?

CHAPTER FIVE

CLAY couldn't keep his eyes off Megan.

After the ceremony he stopped and offered her his arm to exit the church. They parted ways after that—he to do the official wedding stuff he despised and Meg left for the reception hall with her dad. But the moment he entered the Cottonwood Inn for the reception he honed in on her again, standing with Noah and Lily Laramie, a stem glass of pink punch in her hand. Tom Walker approached the group and Clay heard Meg's light laugh as he said something to her. Lord almighty, she was beautiful. How had he not noticed before? He wasn't a fan of short hair; but her simple, sparse style seemed to make her face come alive. Maybe it was makeup—she was wearing the stuff after all, highlighting the sensuous curve of her lips, turning her eyes smoky and mysterious.

Tom moved on, but not before he put his hand along the curve of Meg's back and leaned forward to say something in her ear. Clay frowned as she laughed in response, feeling a spurt of jealousy and pushing it away. He was in trouble. Big, big trouble. His mind was wandering into all sorts of territories just watching her smile and mingle. It was that much worse because it was Meg. Lord knew he hadn't been an angel over the last few years. He'd dated, but he'd stayed away from relationships and always made it clear he wasn't looking for anything permanent.

Even today was torture. He certainly didn't dislike Mike, and he was thrilled his aunt was happy, but the idea of *'til death do us part* always made Clay uneasy. He'd seen how quickly his dad had gone downhill after his mother had abandoned them both. What the cancer hadn't destroyed, her desertion had finished. No one would ever have that much power over Clay. His dad had always been the strong one, but not when it came to her. No, Clay was better off relying on himself.

And now here was Megan, looking irresistible and awakening all of the protective urges he tried to keep locked down. If it were anyone else, he'd consider taking advantage of the situation, enjoying the night with no strings. But there were lines a man didn't cross. Megan Briggs represented more than one of those lines. She was Dawson's sister, she was his friend, and as much as it pained him to admit it, the fact that she'd had cancer scared the daylights out of him. Meg wasn't a one-night-no-strings kind of girl, and it was more than enough to make him take a step back and keep his distance.

They were supposed to be looking out for each other, but Meg didn't exactly look like she needed his help. Instead she looked like a beautiful, exotic flower amidst a bouquet of weeds—and she seemed to be drawing the men's attention like bees to honey.

He should never have asked her here today.

But he had asked her, in a misguided attempt to be there for her like she'd been there for him when times had been tough. He couldn't just back away now and pretend he hadn't. Whatever he was feeling, whatever she'd awakened in him—and it was feeling disturbingly like desire—he would simply lock it away. He'd asked her here as a friend and that was exactly how it was going to be.

He made his way over to her and put on a smile. "I see you made it here just fine."

"I came with Dad." She smiled up at him and that same weird tightening happened again. "He's gone off to talk stock."

"Normally you'd be there with him." Meg wasn't the kind of girl who left the business to the men; she knew what she was about. It was one of the things he truly admired about her.

"Today's not an ordinary day," she replied, taking a sip of punch. His gaze caught on her lips as they touched the glass.

"It certainly isn't," he agreed, but his voice came out low and…dear Lord. Intimate. God. He was no better than Tom Walker with that silly, besotted look on his face. Clay cleared his throat but not before Meg's eyes gleamed with mischief. Great. Bad enough he was reacting to her this way. But to have her notice made him feel ten times the fool.

Lily and Noah moved off to chat with other guests, leaving Meg and Clay alone. Clay made himself forget the way the dress fit her gentle curves and focused on the task at hand. "You seem to be managing okay. No awkward questions, I take it?"

"A few." The flirtatious gleam he'd seen in her eye tempered. "I just keep reminding myself that people mean well. For the most part," she amended, looking at a pair of gray-haired women who were standing by the punch bowl, heads together.

Clay felt a flare of irritation on her behalf, glad to be talking about old ladies rather than besotted young men.

"Some people aren't happy unless they're criticizing or spreading doom and gloom."

Meg lowered her head and he heard an indelicate snort. "Oh, you poor dear. I do hope you *stay* looking so well," she said in a stage whisper.

"They actually said that?" He was appalled.

"Of course. They feed on the possibility of catastrophe," she remarked lightly.

It was no laughing matter to Clay. More than anything he worried about her cancer coming back, not that he'd say so to her face. He wouldn't take away from the happiness of her recovery by admitting such a thing. She was one of the strongest women he knew, and he reached out to take her hand. "Don't you listen to them," he ordered. "You're healthy as a horse and you look beautiful."

"Thank you, Clay." A pretty blush touched her cheeks and his chest swelled.

"I've got your back, remember?"

"I remember," she replied softly, and his heart did a little shiver against his ribs. This wasn't keeping it simple or purely friendly.

"If anyone bothers you, let me know."

"Anyone like who, in particular?" She'd cocked her head to the left, as if trying to figure him out. He clenched his jaw.

"Oh, like Tom Walker. Or Jason Callow. Or…whoever."

"Interesting," she said speculatively, her eyes narrowing as she examined him. He couldn't escape the feeling she was laughing at him on the inside. "Are you jealous, Clay?"

He dropped her hand. "Just wanted you to remember our agreement, that's all." He had to come up with another distraction. "Here's Jen and Andrew," he suggested, tilting his head toward the couple who had just come in. "Good safe people for both of us, right?"

He didn't want to touch her too much so he merely put his hand beneath her elbow as they started across the parlor. Jen and Andrew greeted them with hugs and handshakes and it wasn't long before they were joined by Lily and Noah and Dawson and Tara—the old wing night crowd that Megan had avoided for so long. Now she was a shining star in the midst of them. He couldn't take his eyes off her animated face. How difficult had it been for her to come here tonight? he wondered. However challenging, she'd made more than one conquest already. She looked like a woman who could accomplish anything. He ran a finger over his bottom lip. Offering her his arm tonight was a small favor when all was said and done. He wished there was some way he could help her with her expansion plans. He'd have to give it some thought, see if he could come up with a solution. There was always more than one way to skin a cat.

"You did a wonderful job on the dress," Jen commented to Lily. "You look like a movie star, Meg. I had my doubts about velvet, but you and Lily were right."

"And you were right about the accessories, Jen," Lily said generously. "But Meg, the shoes. The shoes are to die for. Who helped you pick them out?"

Meg grinned. "I picked them out myself." She turned her ankle, showing off the impossibly high slingback heel. Clay's gaze caught on her very fine, toned calf. "I know I'm a bit of a tomboy, but I'm not totally oblivious."

Was she sure about that? Because she seemed to be completely oblivious to what she was doing to Clay with her soft laughs and knockout body. Nothing was working as a distraction. He looked up as Stacy and Mike came through the door, laughing and smiling. Out of the corner of his eye he saw Tom talking to his dad, but with one eye watching Meg constantly. Clay didn't want to leave her side, but he did have official duties to perform. He let his hand rest proprietarily on the small of Meg's back, the heat of her skin warming the velvet against his palm. "They're here," he announced, sounding a little sharper than he intended.

"I need to head back to the kitchen and check up on things," Jen said, handing her empty glass to Drew.

"I suppose we should begin to be seated." Clay put his glass down on a nearby tray. "Meg, you're at the head table with me." There'd be no chance for Tom to move in now.

He saw Tara and Lily exchange significant looks and set his jaw. He hoped they didn't have any ideas of matchmaking. Meg had been right after all. People were seeing a romance where there was none—even if Clay did feel like he'd been hit by lightning. Even if he did feel an absurd need to put his mark on her tonight.

He was in a heck of a jam—being Meg's date, being hugely attracted. He was feeling proprietary and he had no right. It shouldn't matter that Tom had his eye on Meg. Tom was a good guy. But it did bother Clay and that put him on edge, because while he could be friends with Meg it could never be anything more.

It was enough to give him a headache.

Throughout the meal Clay was painfully aware of Meg at his side.

"Could you pass the butter, please?" Meg leaned toward him slightly.

"Oh. Sure." He picked up the dish of perfectly formed butterballs and handed it to her. Their fingers brushed as she took it from him and something strange and electric shot from his fingers to his elbow. Meg's gaze snapped up to his and he took his hand away. The air around them changed as she lowered her eyes and her lips pursed as she carefully put a ball of butter on the side of her plate.

This was not going how he'd planned. He couldn't look at her. He couldn't touch her and yet he didn't want anyone else to, either. How on earth was he going to get through the rest of this evening?

Meg broke a piece off her roll and concentrated on spreading a bit of butter on it so she wouldn't have to look at Clay. What was wrong with him? Granted, she'd wanted to blow him away today and by all accounts she could tell she'd succeeded. Not just with Clay. So many people had been friendly. Heck, Tom Walker had overtly flirted and asked her for a dance later.

But the old teasing Clay was gone and in his place there was an awkward stranger. He couldn't even hand her the butter dish, for heaven's sake! And he'd barely said two words through dinner. She thought back over everything they'd talked about today. There was nothing she could think of that might have made him angry or standoffish. But ever since they'd met up with the rest of the gang he'd closed up tighter than a clam.

"Could you pour me some more wine, please, Clay?" she asked sweetly, lifting her glass. It was still half full but she wanted to try something. As he reached for the bottle, she moved her glass closer until her arm brushed the fine fabric of his white shirt.

He immediately pulled away.

No touching then. Meg pasted on a smile for the table's benefit, said a polite thank-you and took an obligatory sip of the wine even though the liquid had no appeal to her now.

Maybe he'd been momentarily dazzled by her appearance today but the shine had obviously worn off. And maybe she'd let herself believe in the old crush once more—maybe it was the sentimentality of the wedding or something equally foolish—but that wasn't real. She would not make an idiot of herself. And if Clay ended up giving Lisa Hamm a turn on the dance floor tonight, well bully for him. It was no more than he deserved.

When guests rose to get pictures of the couple cutting the cake, she picked up her purse and slid out the side door. It was early April and the wind held a chill; she chafed her arms with her hands and savored the brisk crispness of it. She'd had to escape the perfection. It was all around her today—the romantic setting of the Victorian-style inn, the pretty dresses, the happiness in Lily's eyes and the contentedness she saw in Jen's as Andrew rested a hand on her rounded tummy where their baby grew. It was too much when Meg's life held so much uncertainty. Maybe someday she'd be ready for love, but it wouldn't be easy as a survivor. It stung that everywhere around her were reminders.

It was like starting the game at a deficit, and most of the time she did okay with it. But today the proof lurked in every corner. She rested a hip against the porch railing and looked out over the fields, still dotted here and there with clumps of stubborn snow. *This* was what was real. The ranch land, the herds, the never-changing mountains. This was her life—not the muted laughter and music she heard coming from inside. It had been fun to pretend for a few hours, but the girl in the red dress and high heels and makeup—that wasn't Meg Briggs. That was Meg Briggs trying to prove something. Now that she had, it felt empty.

"Penny for your thoughts."

Clay's voice came from behind her—a surprise. She didn't turn around. "I thought you were avoiding me."

"How could I avoid you when you were sitting right next to me?" He chuckled but she heard the tightness in the sound. She stared at a circling hawk and shrugged.

"It sure seemed like you were trying."

There was a long silence, and then the sound of his boots on the wood floor. "I didn't want people to get the wrong idea."

She got the feeling he wasn't telling the whole truth, but she wasn't sure she wanted to hear it anyway. "And what idea is that?"

"That we're…you know. Together."

Would that really be so bad? She bit back the words. Maybe she'd been wrong about everything today. Maybe the look on his face at the church had just been surprise and not… She thought for a minute. Not what? Attraction? Desire? Boy, she'd really gotten swept up in it, hadn't she? Sure he'd told her she looked beautiful, but wasn't he sort of obligated to say that? His behavior at dinner told the true story. Even if there was something— she'd felt it when their hands brushed—Clay would never admit it. Never act on it. A sound of frustration escaped her throat.

"Are you okay?"

She ground her teeth. "If I had a nickel for every time someone asked me that lately, construction on my riding ring would start within the week."

Clay put his hand on the railing beside her. "For Pete's sake," he said irritably, "it's a simple question and there are lots of ways to be okay. It's not always about…it can just be because you ducked out. You know. Overwhelmed. An emotional thing."

"You can't even say the word, can you?"

She finally turned around and looked up at him. Ah, there it was. The closed expression and the wrinkle above his nose that looked like she could slide a coin into it. He was so afraid of the word *cancer*.

"What do you want from me, Megan?"

The answer rushed into her brain so quickly she had no chance to prepare. *I want you to hold me.* For the first time she truly understood what today was about. It wasn't about showing him. It was about reaching him, something she'd never quite been able to do. He was right here beside her but he'd never been so far away, either.

"Nothing. I don't want anything from you." She went to skirt around him but he reached out and grabbed her wrist.

She looked up at him, feeling her temper rise. "Let go, Clay."

He immediately let go of her wrist, but she didn't run away. "Why are we arguing?"

"I don't know."

"I think you do."

She deliberated telling him exactly what she thought and immediately dismissed the idea. Even if he were ready to hear it—even if she were ready to say it—now was not the time or the place. Not with people around. Not on his aunt's so very special wedding day. She let out a long breath, forced herself to relax. "Let's just enjoy the rest of the wedding, okay? The dancing will be starting up soon."

Which brought out another problem—how could they possibly dance together now, when their emotions were flashing back and forth like a pair of stop and go lights?

"Meg…"

"Not now, Clay." She looked up at him. "Please. Put on a smile and let's go inside. The last thing I need is more people asking if I'm all right. We're supposed to have each other's backs tonight, remember?"

She just wanted to get the evening over with now. When they returned to the banquet room, the tables had been moved aside to make more room on the dance floor. A local DJ was getting ready to start things up and the lights had dimmed.

"Ladies and gentlemen, the bride and groom!"

Meg watched as Stacy and Mike took the floor. Stacy's white dress swirled around her ankles but the true beauty was in her smile. After so many years alone, she'd finally found love and happiness. Meg got a lump in her throat watching them smile and turn through a waltz. Maybe Stacy and Mike were nearing fifty, but they'd seen their chance and they'd taken it. Meg curled her arm around her middle and felt her incision pull just a bit. She doubted that magic would ever happen to her now, doubted she'd ever be ready for it. There were too many uncertainties to contemplate taking such a leap.

After the first dance, Clay danced with Stacy so Meg latched on to Andrew, knowing Jen was finishing up duties in the kitchen. Tom Walker came to claim his dance, and then she circled the floor with Dawson, who point-blank asked her what was going on with Clay.

"Nothing."

"My eye," he responded, swinging her under his arm and bringing her back around.

"You're wrong."

"You knocked his eyeballs out earlier," Dawson said.

"Well, they're back in place now," she replied dryly. "Things are predictably back to normal."

Dawson shook his head. "Clay will never admit it, but he's watching out for you. More than usual. It's like he's everywhere."

She raised an eyebrow. "It's not a real date. Not that anyone is buying that, but it's true." She was still chafing at the idea that Clay felt the need to look out for her.

"I saw his face when he saw you, sis. I'll put money on this being a real date."

"And you obviously have a problem with that."

"Heck, yeah. Clay's my best friend, but that means I know him better than anyone. So do you," he pointed out. "Clay's not the romance kind, Meg. He's a diehard bachelor and we both know why. I can't trust my sister's welfare to a guy who'll end up hurting her, no matter how much I like him."

Trust his sister's welfare? The annoyance of earlier flared back to life. "Oh, you guys," she said sharply, scowling. Dawson slid her under his arm again and she knew it was a deliberate ploy to put her off. When they came face-to-face again she stepped on his foot.

"Ow!"

"Newsflash, Dawson Briggs. I can look after myself. No one needs to watch over me or worry about my welfare. Stop interfering. Got it?"

Dawson muttered something about an ill-tempered snake and she nearly laughed. Nearly.

The song ended and the beat changed to something slow and romantic. Her shoes were new and her feet were beginning to ache but as she turned to leave the dance floor Clay was there, ready to take her into his arms.

"Dance, Squirt?"

She looked him up and down. The bow tie was gone, revealing the delicious V of his neck. His color was up from dancing and he'd rolled up the cuffs of his dress shirt, revealing strong, tapered wrists. As much as she didn't want them to, Dawson's words were too fresh to ignore. Because he was right. Clay had always said he never planned to get married. Even if something did spark between them, she'd be the last woman he'd consider taking on.

"I think I'll sit this one out."

He leaned in and whispered in her ear. "It's a slow dance, Meg. And Lisa Hamm has her radar on full alert."

"So?"

"So we had a deal, remember?" His slow, sexy voice sent ripples over her skin. "Come on, Meg. I promise it won't hurt."

Of course it wouldn't. Clay was as smooth as a twelve-year-old scotch. Meg sighed. It would be far more telling if she refused him than to simply go through with it. "Fine."

He took her hand and led her on to the floor. As he took her in his arms, Meg had the disturbing realization that in all the dances over the years, they'd never slow danced together. As her belly brushed against his cummerbund, she suddenly realized why.

He was holding her close and every inch of her skin was aware of him. Her left breast brushed his shirt and tingled at the contact. There was a certain sadness knowing the same sensation would never happen on the other side—not even if she had reconstruction. As their feet started moving she mourned the changes in her body just a little bit.

This slow dance might be all she ever had with Clay. She didn't want to be protected and babied as he was so determined to do. And the idea of revealing her scars to Clay was preposterous. The woman in the dress was a lie, a fantasy for one day. The scarred, imperfect body was the truth. She was Cinderella at the ball right now, but before long the clock would strike and the dress, the shoes, the makeup would all disappear and she'd still be Meg. Dawson was worrying for nothing.

So she gripped the light fabric of Clay's shirt in her fingers and held on to his hand and closed her eyes. Two things had become so very clear to her today. One, she still cared for Clay way more than she'd thought. And two, she realized that they'd never suit. There was too much between them that was wrong. He wanted to wrap her in bubble wrap; she wanted to fly. He couldn't say the word *cancer;* it was a part of her everyday vocabulary. She was realizing she wanted a husband and a family and Clay would never settle down. There would never be a way for them to meet in the middle.

Even if she wanted them to.

Clay's body was warm and somehow they seemed to meld together. Her head rested on his shoulder and she felt his warm breath against her ear. Neither of them said a word. Neither of them had to. There was something in the dance that spoke for them. An acknowledgment, perhaps, of what was happening between them and what couldn't come of it. A depth of feeling tempered by impossibility.

Meg felt a sting behind her eyes.

The song ended and she pulled away, looking up at Clay. He was looking at her the same way he'd looked today when she'd said hello in the church vestibule. Shocked and aware.

"I think I'd like to go home," she said quietly.

"It'll look…"

"I don't care how it looks." Meg was suddenly so tired of it all. "I just want to go, Clay. Don't worry. You stay. My dad will take me."

Clay took her hand. "No, I will. I asked you to come and I'll drive you home."

Five minutes later they were in his truck heading for the Briggs ranch, and five minutes after that they were at her house. The porch light was on in the spring twilight. Meg opened her door to get out but before she could hop to the ground Clay was there, shutting the door behind her.

"You don't have to walk me to the door."

"Shut up, Meg."

He said it so softly she didn't argue, just listened to their footsteps on the gravel as they walked to the porch door.

"You really were beautiful today," he said, as they lingered just that few extra seconds.

"Don't, okay?" She tried not to choke on the words. She didn't want the crumbs of compliments he was offering. "Thanks for the drive home and good night."

She unlocked the door, but before she could turn the knob his hand covered hers. She turned and froze.

"Clay," she warned, but it was too late.

His arm came around her, lifted her feet clear off the floor as he kissed her: hot, demanding, and all-encompassing.

CHAPTER SIX

His mouth was soft, hot and devastating. Megan let the shock ripple deliciously through her as she clutched his shoulders. There was a small *thunk* as the house key dropped to the step. Even through the layers of his tuxedo and her coat Meg felt the hardness of his body against her.

It was the most wonderful thing she'd felt in her whole life. His lips did terribly skilled things to hers as he moved ahead a step, then another half so that she was pressed against the door with nowhere to go. But the stability meant that she could have her hands free, and once liberated she slid them beneath his lapels and pushed the jacket off his shoulders. His mouth left hers just for a moment and they stood, chests heaving, in the circle of the porch light. Clay's eyes glinted darkly at her as he caught the jacket blindly and draped it in a haphazard clump over the railing.

"Open the door," he commanded, and something seemed to zing from Meg's toes straight to the top of her head. She felt her eyes widen as she understood his intentions; when she said nothing he simply reached around her and turned the knob. She gave a little squeak as his hands spanned her waist and he lifted her over the threshold, kicking the door shut behind him.

"Clay…"

"Be quiet," he commanded, and she swallowed but obeyed. He was looking at her as they stood in the shadows, the only light in the entryway coming from porch light shining through the windows. In the semi-dark he appeared even more dangerous, more forbidden. Mysterious, which to Meg sounded ludicrous consider-ing she'd known him her whole life.

But not this Clay. Not the man who just now was reach-ing out, cupping her head in his wide, capable hand. She wanted this. She'd wanted it for so long, had given up any and all chances of it happening. Maybe another chance would never come. Maybe…she bit down on her lip as she looked at Clay. Cancer had taught her to live each day to the fullest. She was tired of being afraid. His thumb rubbed against her cheek gently. Why shouldn't she take just this much when it was offered?

So she released her lip and tipped her head up, silently inviting him to kiss her again.

He cradled her face in both his hands now and Meg fought for breath as his mouth descended, not with the crash and fury of the first kiss but slowly, deliberately. He took his time now, teasing, tempting, settling into the contact with a sense of inevitability that rocked her world and made her yearn for far more than a good-night kiss or a single night to remember.

"I've wanted to do this all day," he confessed, and Meg's body came alive hearing the soft but urgent words. His mouth was on hers again, making her weak in the knees. She pushed away the warning that sounded in her head when Clay lowered his hands and unbuttoned her coat. It was just a coat. It was fine. She let it fall to the floor and curled a hand around his neck, pulling him closer, tasting. He tasted like the chocolate mousse from the dessert, flavored with a hint of tart raspberry coulis.

Clay slid one hand over her left shoulder and down, his fingertips sliding over her breast. At first Meg shuddered, feeling utterly feminine and sexual for the first time in months. But as Clay made an impassioned sound in his throat Meg came to her senses. He didn't know, couldn't know what surgery had cost her. It was too risky, too frightening. What if he'd used the other hand? He would have slid his fingers over something that wasn't real. Clay mattered. For the sake of their friendship, it had to stop here.

She pushed against him, making enough room that she could slide past his body and into the warmth of the kitchen. She hugged her arms around herself. How could she have forgotten so easily? Meg felt the color drain from her face as her body chilled. It was an embarrassment she had no desire to endure.

"Meg." Clay followed her into the kitchen. Just the way he said her name, soft but with a bit of wariness, put her on edge.

"I can't do this," she said quietly, knowing he had no idea how much saying it was tearing her apart. The peace she'd made—with herself, with her disease—evaporated, leaving her angry and full of self-loathing. Now, when she finally had what she'd always wanted in her grasp, *who* she wanted, she had to push him away. "You don't want this," she said, stronger now. "You don't want me. You should go."

He reached over and turned on the kitchen light, flooding them in brightness. Meg hated the glare. Hated the idea of being so *visible*, inside and out.

"What the hell just happened?" He frowned at her, his expression a mix of frustration and confusion.

Meg knew what he meant and deliberately misunderstood. "Why don't you tell me? You were the one who insisted on walking me to the door. Who wouldn't let me open…"

"That's not what I mean."

She looked away. There was irritation in his eyes but there was something more. Clay looked *hurt*. How could that be? "Why did you kiss me?" she asked, lifting her chin. Anything to keep him from searching for the real answer to his question. Anything but the humiliation of having to explain.

"Because I wanted to," he replied.

They were both stubborn but Meg was no fool. "Now who's deliberately dodging? You know what I'm asking. Why did you *want* to?"

He took a step closer and Meg backed away, skirting around the table and putting it between the two of them. Clay's face looked suddenly tired. "Good Lord, Meg. I'm not going to hurt you."

But he would. He would if she let herself believe in this fantasy. She knew his reasons and it was all her fault. He had to know them, too. Had to say them so he could see how foolish it all was. "Why did you want to kiss me, Clay?" She repeated the question, her hands braced on the back of the chair before her.

"Look at you," he admitted roughly. "You walked through the church today and every eye was on you. You have to know that."

"So it's just physical?"

"Of course not!" His shoulders straightened.

She was relieved and not relieved at the same time. If it wasn't just physical, then there was more. Friends with benefits? She knew Clay too well for that. He had to see how wrong this was. Even as her lips still hummed from his kiss, she knew in her heart that in the end someone was going to get hurt. Or both of them. "So you have feelings for me," she dared.

Clay paused. "It's not that simple."

She knew it wasn't, and that was the point. "Because if you're going with physical attraction—" she braced herself for the next words, knowing they had to be said "—you're going to be sorely disappointed."

"What are you talking about?" His gaze darkened. "Don't tell me you don't feel it, too. I felt you in my arms. You practically melted." He put his hands on his hips. "I might have started it, but you were right there with me. And then you pushed me away like I did something wrong. Unforgivable."

He really didn't know. She let that bit sink in for a few moments, trying to figure out where to go from here. It explained a lot. She'd guarded the details of her treatment well, and so had her family. The knowledge warmed her just a bit. They'd stood behind her even when what she'd asked hadn't been easy.

Clay truly didn't know the extent of her surgery. She had to think about how to say it just right.

"This…" She swept her hand down at her dress. "This is not the real me, Clay. It was a mistake for me to pretend. You asked me to go with you and I had some silly idea to go all out and prove a point. But the makeup and dress and high heels…it's an act. If you'd left me at the door I'd be in flannel sleep pants and a T-shirt by now."

"And that'd be sexy as hell," he answered. "Good God, Meg, give me some credit. I've known you for years. I know this isn't normal for you. Maybe that's why it hit me so hard." He smiled, a sexy little upturn of his lips. "Discovering you're a girl was more than I bargained for."

"I don't want…"

The smile faded. "Don't want me? You did a damn good job making it seem like you did."

Frustration began to bubble. "Stop finishing my sentences. You've got it all wrong, don't you see? It's not just the dress that's not me, it's...it's..."

Her lip wobbled. He truly hadn't seen her as a woman until today. And it had taken her pretending to be someone else to make it happen. She felt old dreams shatter, the pieces dropping around her feet. Clay would never love her, and she had to stop this insanity now. If she couldn't have all of him, she at least wanted to keep his friendship.

"Dawson said this would be a mistake."

Clay's eyes glittered dangerously. "Leave your brother out of this."

Meg ran her tongue over her lips. "But I can't, Clay, because he was right." It pained her to admit it but it was true. She swallowed, blinked, breathed. "We don't want the same things, and I'm not prepared to take any gambles right now. The Meg who went away...not all of her came back. There are parts of me that'll never come back. Some more obvious than others."

She pressed a hand to her right breast and saw the moment Clay understood. Any teasing, any sexual frustration he had been feeling fled and he looked both fascinated and horrified.

"You mean...all of it?"

"Yes. No lumpectomy. Full mastectomy, and a few lymph nodes for good measure."

His ruddy cheeks blanched. "So you...I mean..."

He was so uncomfortable that she felt pity for him. But she'd been right to push away. What if he'd touched her without realizing? It would have been too humiliating. No matter what anyone said, a breast form was far from the same thing. Not for him and not for her. And judging by his reaction now, the only thing she would share were the words. He could barely handle those. He wouldn't be able to handle the scars, or the sight of her as less of a woman. The idea of letting herself be that vulnerable and watching him turn away nearly stole her breath. She couldn't do it.

"I wear a prosthetic—a form inside my bra."

Clay uttered a curse word, pulled out a chair and sat down.

Meg let out her breath. She'd said it. She pulled out the chair beneath her hands and sat across from him. "When we were outside tonight, at the inn, I said you couldn't say the word. If you can't say it, Clay, you can't handle this. And so I stopped you before it could blow up in our faces. You got caught up in it today, just like me, that's all. You'll thank me later."

She wanted to believe that was true, but all she wanted was to feel his arms around her again. He wasn't the only one who got more than he bargained for today.

"I can say it," Clay protested, his lips a thin, grim line. "I just didn't think you wanted to hear it. You hate it when people bring up your illness. You want to pretend it didn't happen."

It was only a partial truth. She did hate it, but she was right. He hated cancer. He *was* afraid of it. It was merciless and didn't discriminate. Tonight he'd wanted to forget about it. Meg was so gorgeous, so alive in his arms. When she'd rested her head on his shoulder as they'd danced she'd started something that he'd finished on her porch step. He was attracted to Megan Briggs and he'd conveniently forgotten all the reasons why he should stay away. He hadn't been able to help himself from taking her in his arms, kissing her. It was the damnedest thing. What shook him right to the bottom of his shoes was that it felt so *right*.

It had felt like everything was clicking into place until the moment she'd frozen in his arms. In a way he was glad she'd put on the brakes. The last thing Clay wanted was to play games with Meg, and what else could it possibly be? He wasn't interested in anything serious, and it was impossible to be anything else with Meg. He knew her too well. They'd shared too many secrets as friends. That type of connection wasn't something he could be careless with.

As he looked at her now, he knew it was more than just their friendship on the line, too. Meg was scared. For all her protests to the contrary, Meg was still scared to death and pushing her into something based on hormones and attraction would only hurt them both. He had to tread very, very carefully so that nothing was broken irreparably.

"I could never pretend it didn't happen." She folded her hands on the table. "The experience is a part of who I am now. The trouble starts when people think that's *all* I am."

"You had cancer, Meg. You could have died." She hadn't, but the spectre was always there. "People worry about you. I worry about you, okay? I don't want to lose another person I..."

Her head came up and her gaze pierced his. "You what?"

"I care about," he finished. He wanted to think that what she'd revealed tonight didn't matter. That he didn't care about scars, that he was a bigger man. But in his head he kept seeing the surgeon's knife and it made him feel light in the stomach. She was right. It was better that they stop things right where they were. She might think it was about her scars but for Clay it was so much more. He had his own scars to deal with, the kind that didn't leave physical proof. And now those scars were somehow tied to the one person he was coming to realize he'd always counted on. Her.

Tonight he'd nearly ruined everything by getting carried away. If it meant letting her believe he was repulsed by her appearance, he'd take the hit to his character. It was difficult enough being her friend, but it was nothing compared to being her lover. Friends…lovers…two very, very different things carrying vastly different risks. Love changed things. Love was like taking your heart out of your body and putting it in someone else's keeping. It required a faith he didn't possess.

"I understand," he said quietly. "If you're okay, I should go."

"Of course I'm fine."

Of course she was. Meg would never admit any differently, would she? He pushed away from the table and the chair legs grated against the floor, unusually loud in the awkward silence. He went to the door and she followed him, picking up her coat and hanging it on a hook while he paused with a hand on the doorknob.

"I'm sorry, Meg." He was sorry for a lot of things and he hoped she'd let it go at that and not ask him to elaborate. He made himself meet her eyes. She was watching him with such soft understanding he felt about two inches tall. A coward.

"It's okay," she answered. "It's a lot to handle. I knew it and I let things get out of hand."

She was blaming herself? He stepped forward. "Not your fault. Not even a little bit, understand?"

Her cheeks blossomed prettily and Clay's gaze dropped

to her lips. But her breath had quickened and he saw the rise and fall of her chest. No, they had to leave things as they were. They had to stay friends for everyone's sake. "Let's just forget about it," he murmured, opening the door.

"Good idea," she answered.

He leaned forward and gave her a light peck on the cheek. "Good night, Meg."

But she didn't answer as she shut the door behind him and he collected his tux jacket from the railing. Night had fallen completely and April stars were gleaming in a cold sky.

Maybe he should have stayed. He wasn't proud of himself and he couldn't help but think of his mother as he started the truck. She hadn't been able to handle his father's illness and had left them both. He'd always considered her weak and unfeeling. He'd always been so very determined not to be like her.

Now Meg undoubtedly thought he was, and he was surprised to find that it hurt. Her opinion mattered to him. For the first time in his life he realized that the real motivations behind his parents' split were possibly different than he'd always thought. After holding Meg in his arms, he found it possible to believe that his mother had loved his father but hadn't had the strength to handle watching him die.

It was no excuse, but Clay understood it. And he hated himself for it.

Meg rubbed Calico's neck as she let the mare walk to cool down. A year of inconsistent exercise had both of them out of shape, and she was toying with the idea of doing one more season before hanging up her rodeo hat for good. She had to have something other than the day-to-day running of the ranch. Maybe she just needed to do this one step at a time. Save what she could and build piece by piece.

She sat tall in the saddle, looking at the barrels. Trouble was, as good as she was at racing, she'd never felt like the rodeo royalty type and another year of the circuit sounded exhausting. Somewhere along the way she'd lost her competitive edge. Or perhaps she'd spent so much energy fighting her cancer that she simply didn't want to compete anymore. The last few days she'd been listless, unsettled. She told herself it had nothing to do with Clay but it did.

He'd disappointed her.

She had wanted him to proclaim that it didn't matter. That her scars meant nothing. Not that it would have changed anything, but she'd wanted to hear him say it anyway. He hadn't. She had been so right about stopping things before they truly got started. Now she just wished they could go back to the way things were before.

But they couldn't and thinking about it was hurting her brain. Calico tossed her head. What Meg really wanted to do this morning was ride. Forget about everything but the feel of the saddle and the wind in her hair. Calico was done for the day, so Meg rubbed her down and turned her loose. It was Dawson's mount she turned to as the spring sun spread its light down the barn corridor. She saddled up his gelding, Enforcer, instead.

Enforcer pulled at the bit until Meg had him outside the farmyard, and then she let him have his head. She gave a whoop as he leaped forward, eating up the earth with long strides. This was what she needed—full on, no-holds-barred. For several minutes they headed north along the fence line, then turned east along the creek that bordered Briggs' land and Gregorys'. In the distance she could see small brown dots on the burgeoning green grass—Clay's herd. Far ahead of her was a lone rider. She didn't need to see his face to know who it was. Clay Gregory had a way of sitting a horse that was all his own.

Clay. Her heart did a little jump and settle thing every time she thought of him. She had been wrong trying to prove something to him considering how it had turned out. And yet she couldn't quite bring herself to regret it. Not when the few minutes in his arms had been so completely glorious. She'd hold the memory close for a long, long time no matter what happened.

She could tell when he spotted her—he straightened in the saddle and he altered his path, coming straight for her. She locked down the excitement that raced through her veins. Just because he sat a horse prettier than anyone she knew, just because...

Oh, forget it. It was a pointless exercise.

"Problems?" she called out as he approached.

Clay reined in and Meg admired not only rider but Sir Winston, Clay's mount. "Sir," as they called him, was jet-black and had the bones and chest of a quarter horse and the height of a Thoroughbred. He was a giant, smart and even-tempered. Clay never let anyone ride Sir other than himself.

"Just checking out the fence line." He nudged closer to her and looked down at her from beneath his hat. "You?"

"Just out for a ride. I thought you'd have a quad for this stuff."

"Dawson likes his toys. I still like horse work."

Meg's lips twitched. Clay would deny it all day long but in many ways he really was old-school. She liked that about him. Clay never got caught up in new and shiny things. He was steady, reliable.

Predictable, she realized, her mood sinking. He had

reacted exactly as she'd expected, so why did she fault him for it? "I'll let you get back to it, then." She turned Enforcer about and faced home.

"Something wrong with Calico?"

She stopped and twisted in the saddle to look back at him. "No, why?"

"You're on Enforcer, that's all."

"I was working Calico this morning and gave her a rest."

Clay's face changed, turning speculative. "Working her?"

"I'm considering doing one more season."

"Is that what you want?"

Meg sighed, reined her horse lightly and went back to face him. Perhaps Clay had found it easier than she had to forget the other night. He was certainly adept at making conversation today as if she had never melted in his arms. "Not in a perfect world," she answered. "But I haven't been able to find a way to make the stables happen. I considered asking if we could sell off a parcel, but the truth is, other than what we've rented out, we need every acre for a herd our size and I know it. And that's a sacrifice the family would have to make for me, which isn't what I want. But I have to do something with my time. So I'll do one last season while I figure it out, I guess."

She knew she sounded less than thrilled and Clay's frown confirmed it.

"Ride with me," he suggested. "I've been thinking and I might have a solution for you."

"Will I like it?"

"Probably not." He flashed a grin, reminding her of the old, easygoing Clay. Maybe they could put their mistake behind them. It was what she wanted. But she missed the hot gleam in his eyes now that she'd experienced it aimed in her direction. She'd have to find a way to ignore that.

"Then why am I listening?"

He laughed. "Because it solves your problem."

Meg wasn't convinced it was a good idea, but the tiny flash of hope she felt at his words couldn't be ignored. She turned Enforcer around so she and Clay were side by side.

"You mind if we ride along this fence line?" Clay nodded at the pasture on their right. "I haven't finished checking it yet, and I want to move the herd in a few days."

The two families' land bordered each other all along this side and the idea of trespassing was completely foreign. Meg shrugged. "Wouldn't hurt for me to have a look, either. I don't know when Dawson was out last. If he's not in the fields he's in town *courting*."

"Things are getting serious with Tara," he stated.

"It looks that way."

They picked their way along the property line. Clay cleared his throat and Meg looked over at him. The other night she'd been able to read his face. Today she couldn't. He'd closed it off completely.

"I've been thinking, and I know of a way you can raise the capital to start your business. I want to loan you the money for the ring and stable," he said.

Meg nearly fell off her horse. Then she began laughing, the sound ringing in the air. Lord, no one had that kind of money just laying around doing nothing! "Oh, Clay, that's funny. Let's go raid your penny jar."

"I'm not joking."

She stopped laughing. His jaw was set like a chunk of glacier granite dropped in the middle of the prairie. He was serious. Dead serious. It had to be a joke. Because if he meant it she got the uneasy feeling it was tainted somehow. Was he feeling guilty? Or was he trying to prove something? Either way, Meg didn't like that it felt like he was playing a game, with her future at the middle of it.

"Where would you get that kind of money? I know your place is doing okay, but it's not *that* kind of ranch, Clay. We both know that."

"If I did have the money, would you take it?"

Temptation squeezed her heart. She didn't want money from Clay. She didn't know what she wanted, but the idea that he might think he had to buy her friendship stung. And yet if she took the money—if it was really offered— it could solve all her problems. "I don't know."

His shoulders relaxed. "You want to."

A sudden idea hit her. "You're not thinking of taking on any debt for this, are you? Because that would be an 'absolutely not.'" Why on earth was he offering this to her now? She'd told him about the idea weeks ago. Unless…

She was right. He had to be feeling guilty. Or scared.

"I don't want sympathy money," she said sharply, gripping the reins almost painfully.

Clay made a disparaging sound in his throat. "God, woman! You make it near impossible for anyone to help you. You think everyone's motives are exactly what you don't want, and then you feel very self-satisfied when you're proven right."

She could feel his glare on her, sharp and accusing. Had she misjudged him? She was barely wrapping her mind around it when he spoke again, his voice harsh and unrelenting.

"You know what, Meg? I do pity you. Because the one dwelling on your cancer is you. You make it an issue no matter what. You're afraid. No one should see any sort of weakness in Meg Briggs. Well, here's a tidbit. You don't have to be perfect. No one is, and no one expects it."

"Yes, they do!" she shouted, and her voice echoed down the valley and over the creek.

Clay pulled Sir Winston to a stop and twisted in the saddle. She looked up into his face, half-shadowed by his Stetson. Lord, no matter what justifications she made in her head, she still wanted him. Still cared for him so very much. And he understood nothing. Nothing about the pressure she was under. Nothing about how to come to grips with it all herself while putting a smile on her face for everyone else's benefit. She was one of the lucky ones. She should be counting her blessings rather than thinking about her losses. She knew it, but, oh, sometimes it was hard.

And he knew nothing about how their error in judgment the other night had opened the door to a dream and then slammed it shut again.

"I have to hold myself together and them, too," Meg said, quieter now.

Her heart was pounding and there was a sinking feeling in her stomach but she fought to ignore it. He couldn't be right. He wasn't right. She'd beaten cancer. She'd moved beyond. Why couldn't he see that? "I feel like I'm walking a tightrope and I have to be bouncy and happy and energetic all the time. It's exhausting, Clay. One slip and I'm off the tightrope and falling. I can't stand it. I can't stand the worry on Mom's face or the strain on Dawson's or the guilt on Dad's. He would do anything to be back out there with Dawson and me again. And all of them are looking to me, don't you see? So don't you dare tell me no one expects me to be perfect! Because if I'm not they're absolutely terrified. I mean look at you.

A few words from me the other night and you couldn't get out of the house fast enough!"

Clay looked at her for one long, torturous moment. She wanted him to say something. To disagree with her. Anything but the cold silence he was giving her.

But there was nothing. With a kick of his heels, he spurred Sir Winston on.

And he never looked back.

CHAPTER SEVEN

THE last thing Meg wanted to do was knock on Clay's door and face him, but she did it. She rapped her knuckles three times on the screen door and stepped back.

Meg hated admitting she was wrong. But she'd ridden around on Enforcer for an hour thinking about what he'd said. He was right. She was standing in her own way and she needed to get out of it if she wanted to succeed. More than that, she'd been particularly nasty in her parting words and she was sorry for it.

She saw him through the screen as he came to the door. Saw the surprised look on his face as he approached and how he tried to hide it. He hadn't expected her to come. He'd expected her to run home with her tail between her legs.

She was happy to disappoint him, at least this time. But she still noticed the long length of his legs, the firm breadth of his chest, his tanned face. She wished the old longings had never been resurrected, but it looked like they were here to stay and somehow she had to deal with it.

He opened the door and held it.

"Can I come in?"

He stepped aside.

She went inside and shoved her hands inside the front

pouch of her hoodie. He hadn't said a word—perhaps during the hour she'd spent thinking he'd been nursing his anger. He certainly seemed to have a lot of it. Maybe he'd simply given up on her. Her stomach did a little flip. "I turned my horse out with Sir. Hope that's okay."

Clay's jaw tightened. "That's fine."

They'd done such a thing tons of times in the past, so the fact that she'd asked for his approval felt weird—and the terse answer even stranger. Meg struggled to find words. "I rode around for a while and ended up here," she said, as if it explained everything.

Clay nodded at her feet. "Take off your boots then and come in." He hesitated. "I just took out a steak. Can take another out if you want."

He walked to the kitchen, leaving her to follow.

The invitation was hardly heartfelt, and Meg wondered if she'd made a mistake coming here. But things were bubbling between her and Clay and they needed to clear the air. The words they'd shouted today couldn't be left to fester. Even if they'd backed off from anything romantic, the last thing Meg wanted was the complete disintegration of their friendship. Friends were too valuable a commodity to discard without a thought. After all these years they just had to try harder.

"Mom will be expecting me," she called, shoving off her boots and leaving them by the door. She padded down the hall in her stocking feet, knowing that staying for dinner was a temptation she didn't need. "The joys of living at home," she said, forcing her voice to sound light and cheery as she entered the cozy kitchen. "One of these days I'll have to see about getting my own place."

"I think that'd be good for you."

Clay stood at the sink as he scrubbed a potato. Meg noticed that it was fairly tidy considering he was living here alone now without Stacy to keep things on track in the house. Meg had always liked his home. It wasn't big but it was comfortable, and Stacy had always ensured that people felt welcome in it. This moment was probably the most uncomfortable Meg had ever felt within its walls.

"I think it would be good for me, too." She picked up the thread of what he'd last said. The idea of having her own space was more attractive than he could imagine, yet another one of the things on her list she simply couldn't afford. She paused and Clay put down the potato and picked up another. She really needed to apologize and get it over with. "Are you going to look at me, Clay?"

He did. She knew her hair was standing up on one side from the wind and her face felt ruddy and chapped from the cold, but she stood her ground. She remembered the way he'd looked at her in her red dress. The difference was clear. The real Meg was right in front of him, in jeans and a navy hoodie and stockinged feet. As ordinary as ditch water. And Clay wore old jeans and a gray T-shirt—a complete departure from his debonair tuxedo. But now she knew. She knew the sound of his breathing in the dark. The taste of him. The way he cupped her face, at once gentle and commanding. They were supposed to go back to the way things were before, but for Meg it was impossible. The best she could hope for was amity. Perhaps understanding. She needed Clay. He was the only one who'd been completely honest with her since her return—even when it hurt. There was no pretending with him, not anymore.

"I'm sorry," she said, her gaze not leaving his. "I'm sorry for shouting at you and unloading on you."

Clay's tongue came out to wet his lips and he opened his mouth to say something, hesitated and finally said,

"I didn't mean to go off like that, either. I just want to help."

"You were honest with me, Clay. It was hard to hear. But I rode around a long time being angry and thinking about what you said. My feelings aren't wrong. I do feel like I have to be perfect. But you're right that I'm getting in my own way."

"You're putting so much pressure on yourself. But your family—your true friends—are big boys and girls. We can handle it."

She met his gaze, knowing she had to say all the words she'd thought while riding over the fields. "I want to think that. But if I admit a weakness to them, I might have to admit it to myself, you see?"

And admitting weakness meant letting in fear. How could she do that? She'd spent months being strong, looking forward toward the only acceptable goal—recovery. "I don't know how to be vulnerable. I don't know how to deal with the worried looks on their faces if I have so much as a headache. I don't know how to do it, Clay. Sometimes I want to scream. Can you imagine if I just let loose? Mother wouldn't know what to do with herself." She fiddled her fingers around each other. "I thought beating this thing would make the rest of it easy, but it's not at all, and I can't seem to figure it out. And that's why I yelled at you this afternoon and I'm sorry."

"That couldn't have been easy for you to say," he said quietly, putting down the potato and wiping his hands on a dishcloth. "I was too hard on you. I owe you an apology, too. I was just…frustrated."

Frustrated. She knew the meaning of that word. Ever since he'd kissed her the frustration within her only seemed to build, putting her more on edge. Unsatisfied. Off balance. It was shocking to think that along with everything else she was feeling sexual frustration. Was it the same for him? It didn't seem to be. He seemed absolutely calm and in control.

"I did scream today," she admitted. "Once. When I was sure you were out of earshot."

Clay chuckled way down low, and it sent a delicious spiral rippling through her body. "And how did you feel, afterward?" he asked.

"Ridiculous," she admitted, and suddenly the angry tension surrounding them dissipated, adding a level of comfort. But these days being comfortable together held a tension all its own. Dancing with Clay, kissing Clay—it had changed everything. At least for her. What pushed them apart before was now drawing them together.

He picked up the potatoes again and put them in the oven. "You're spinning your wheels, that's all."

"Yes." It felt so good to say it. "And then the other night, at the wedding, I felt so in control. But it was an illusion." Them being together was an illusion, too. It hurt to admit it; but it was the truth.

"Things got screwed up," he said, but his voice took on a husky quality. Meg looked into his eyes and felt such a strong pull to walk into his arms, to rest there for a little while. Even after all that had happened—how absolutely messed up it all was, she wished she could just do that. Be safe in the circle of his arms for a minute or two.

"I still want to build this expansion," she said, clearing her throat. They had to get back on track before she did something really stupid. It was, after all, the real reason she was here. She wanted to hear what he had to say. "I jumped all over you before instead of listening. If you have a solution, I'd like to hear it. And make a rational decision." She smiled up at him. There was no need to admit she'd been emotional—she knew she'd been all over the map.

Clay gestured toward the table with a hand. "Then have a seat and let's talk."

His mind spun as he went to the fridge to grab a couple of drinks and gather his thoughts. He hadn't meant to say all that to Meg in the meadow. He'd thought long and hard about his offer and how best to present it to her. But she hadn't even heard him out. She'd thrown out the pity word and he'd lost it. Told her exactly what he thought and the hell with sparing her feelings.

Feelings, ha. He had asked himself plenty of times over the last few days what he wanted from Megan. Each time the answer had come back—and it was always an answer he didn't want to hear. He couldn't want *love*. He didn't want her to love him and he didn't want to love her. There were too many risks involved.

The problem was he was already in over his head. If it had just been a fancy dress and a fine pair of legs in high heels he could have moved on, just as he'd always done. A flirtation was fine but he never let himself get serious about anyone. But this was Meg. She was different. It didn't matter if she was dressed to the nines or like she was today—adorable and oh-so approachable in her jeans and soft sweatshirt. He knew her inside and out— why else would she make him so angry? He couldn't just hold her in his arms and walk away. He had to be careful.

But he also knew it would never work. He wasn't the marrying kind. Dawson called him The Bachelor like the reality TV show of the same name, and quipped him about whether or not he was going to institute his own rose ceremony to send the ladies on their way when he broke their hearts. For a long time Clay had laughed at

the comparison. But lately it had been wearing thin—
both the name and the meaningless dating.

And Meg was…

Well. Meg was a mess and she deserved better than
him. She deserved someone who would be there for her
in ways that he couldn't. The last thing he wanted to do
was complicate things further when she was struggling
so much. The idea of opening his heart to her only to
have it tramped on was not the most attractive option
on the table. It would end badly, no doubt about it. So,
yeah, maybe he was feeling the smallest bit guilty about
Saturday night. He'd started something that could never
be finished.

All he knew was that he valued her friendship too
much to mess around with it. Loaning her money was
the one thing he could truly do to help, while at the same
time keeping his heart wrapped up nice and safe.

He took out two cans of pop and put one in front of
her; then he took a seat, popping the top of the can. He
looked at her from across the table and wondered how
to broach the subject better this time, so she didn't see it
as some pity party.

"Look, Meg. I know that if it weren't for bank poli-
cies you'd already be on your way to making this a reality. Clearly you're strong and healthy, right?" He ignored
the niggling voice in his head that persisted in chirping
about risks and reoccurrence rates. "And you know what
you're doing. You've been around horses all your life.
It's a crying shame that you keep coming up against the
word no."

She couldn't argue with any of that, he reasoned. She
took a drink of her pop and said nothing, which was encouraging.

"The only thing keeping this from going ahead is capital. I have it. It's yours."

He watched as Meg's finger circled the lip of the can. Finally she looked up at him. "This isn't about feeling guilty about the other night?"

Her question was aimed true and he took the hit. He pushed his pop aside, swallowing roughly. "Guilty?"

He had felt guilt. About letting her mistakenly believe he was turned off by the changes in her body. About losing control and hurting her. But enough to want to make restitution with money?

"Pardon me," he said dryly, "but I hardly think that what happened between us is cause for *that* much guilt. And I'm a little insulted that you think I'd try to buy you off." Even as he said it he felt the little slide of uneasiness knowing he still wasn't being completely truthful. But how on earth could he say, "I can't love you as you should be loved so here's your consolation prize"?

"Okay, okay. I didn't mean to imply…" Her eyes looked distressed and she moved to tuck her hair behind her ear, only it wasn't long enough. She was nervous. They'd never been nervous around each other before. "I'll shut up now," she whispered, and Clay let out a breath. He didn't want to fight with her. Somehow they had to find their feet. Put things on an even keel again.

"This is a friend to friend offering, Meg. Neighbor to neighbor. I want you to have it."

"As a loan," she said.

Clay ran his hand over his hair. She wasn't going to make this easy, was she? Why couldn't she just accept it as a gift and go?

Because she was Meg. Because, to a certain extent she was right. People did count on her. Meg always paid her way. She always did things right. Maybe she *had* felt more pressure than any of them had realized so they could all feel a bit more secure, reassured. She could hardly be responsible for everyone's feelings, could she?

"I meant it as a gift, but you won't accept it that way, will you?"

She shook her head. Her face was uncompromising and she coolly took another drink. He felt like smiling then. She was a heck of a negotiator, even when she didn't have the upper hand.

"I want to know how you happen to have all this money lying around. And why you haven't put it into your own place." Her brows pulled together. "Any farmer worth his salt either puts his money back into the operation, or it's his rainy-day safety net if the worst happens."

Clay pursed his lips. The story was old history, especially now that Stacy was gone, but he still held the resentment deep in his heart. He hadn't even wanted to accept the money to begin with, but Stacy had convinced him, telling him it would come in handy someday. The irony wasn't lost on him. His mother had left it to him and it had felt like a payoff for all the love she'd deprived him of as a boy. Now he was offering it to Meg instead of offering himself. He could never confess such a shortcoming to her.

"Does it matter where it came from?"

Meg's dark eyes cooled. "It matters to me, Clay. It really matters. You know I can't take any money that will compromise your ranch. It wouldn't be right."

She wouldn't let it go. He'd have to tell her, but he'd keep to the unemotional facts. "It was my mother's," he replied. He folded his hands and leaned forward. "She left it to me."

"That still doesn't explain…"

"I don't want my mother's money touching this place,"

he said sharply. Too sharply perhaps, because Meg's shoulders stiffened. But he and Stacy had gone through this time and again and it was something he felt strongly about. His mother had never wanted this farm. She'd never wanted him when all was said and done. Maybe she had loved his father, maybe she hadn't, but the painful truth was either way she'd left her kid behind. He hadn't given a damn about her money. At one time he'd have given it all for a simple acknowledgment.

"But it's okay to give to me. For it to 'touch' the Briggs ranch." She shook her head. "I don't understand, Clay."

How did he explain that it felt tainted to him without insulting her at the same time? "Money is money, Meg. It's not that there's anything wrong with it. She left it to me when she died a few years back. That was all I got, you realize. Legal correspondence. Not once in the years since she walked away did she contact me. Anything this ranch has become is in spite of her and not because of her. Stacy thought I was crazy, but I couldn't bring myself to use it. In the end I invested it."

She reached over and took his hand. The contact rippled through his fingers and along the length of his arm, settling hard in the center of his body. But he didn't pull his hand away. He didn't want her to know what the simple touch did to him. For a few moments he was eleven years old again, back in the meadow, wiping his eyes on the back of his sleeve as Meg put her hand in his and said, "Don't worry, Clay. I won't ever leave you. Promise."

Neither of them ever spoke of that afternoon again, but it had been in the front of his mind when she'd said the words *breast cancer*. From that moment he had failed to live up to the tacit promise he'd made when he'd squeezed her hand in return. Helping her now was the best way he could think of to make up his past failings.

"I'm not as angry as I was," he said, and realized it was true. "It just didn't feel right when she never loved this place, you know? It should do some good somewhere. I don't know why I didn't think of it in the first place. This could fix everything. I want you to have this chance, Meg. I believe in you."

Meg gripped his fingers firmly as tears gathered in the corners of her eyes. "You never talk about your mother. Never," she whispered.

"You pushed."

Yes, she had, and she felt bad about it and yet somewhat relieved. She wouldn't have accepted her family going into debt for her and she wouldn't have accepted those terms from Clay, either. But what a thing for him. What a slap in the face. For all her family's faults, for all their stifling, worried glances, she had never once felt unloved or unwanted.

In all the years growing up it had been an unspoken rule: you don't talk about Clay's parents. But Meg knew the story and she could understand his resentment.

"I understand you want to have something positive come from the money." He was handing her the opportunity she craved, like a sweet in front of a child and she was afraid to reach out and take it. The fact that he believed in her made her heart sing. Now, faced with the prospect of making it a reality, she wasn't quite sure she believed in herself.

She slipped her fingers from his and curled them around her pop can. It was hard to believe there wasn't a little bit of guilt at play in his sudden offer. She remembered the look on his face when he'd realized she was missing a breast. She'd told herself that it was a perfectly normal reaction but the truth was she'd wanted more—expected more—from Clay. But maybe that was the problem. Maybe they expected too much from each other. After all, what had happened between them was nothing disastrous. Nothing worth ruining a whole friendship over. And while she had reservations—borrowing money from friends could really be a recipe for disaster—the carrot he was dangling before her was too bright and shiny to resist.

She sat back in her chair. "If I borrow the money, I have complete autonomy over the operation. The construction, the operation, everything. You have no say."

His gaze was keen on her. "Did I imply otherwise?"

She could see it in her mind. The warm summer breeze carrying the voices and laughter of children. The stable full of healthy horses, a riding ring set up with barrels or being circled by new riders.

Her own business. Her own contribution. And business partners with Clay. Her balloon popped. Because no matter what he said, he could never be the silent kind of partner.

That idea made her throat close over. She could just hear her father's voice saying that business partners made for bad bedfellows. If he only knew how close she and Clay had come to the latter he'd give her one of those disapproving looks she despised. They couldn't be partners.

And he was agreeing to it all too easily. She bit down on her lip, wondering what the pill in the jam would be. "I know you, Clay. You'll put in your two cents. You're not capable of keeping your opinion to yourself."

"So you are going to close your mind to helpful advice? Are you sure that's wise?"

"There's a difference between helpful advice and taking over. You'll make noises about protecting your investment and all that nonsense." He would, too. This would

bind them together for a long time. It would be years before she could pay off the entire loan. She would be tied
to Clay for ages—except for the one way she wanted to
be tied to him. Exchanging one dream for another. She
supposed it wasn't a bad sort of thing, so why wasn't she
happier?

Clay got up from the table and walked to the window
looking out over the backyard. Meg's insides twisted. His
shoulders were tense and he'd shut her out by turning his
back on her. She'd made him angry again. With a sigh
she put her forehead on her hand. She seemed to insult
him without trying. She'd walked through the door determined to get out of her own way and here she was right
back at it again, throwing up excuses rather than finding
solutions. No wonder Clay got frustrated with her.

Finally Clay turned back around. "Meg, you need to
decide what it is you want. I'm offering you an answer
to all your worries, and still you're finding reasons why
not. What are you so afraid of? No one is throwing up
roadblocks but you. My offer stands, but you're under
no obligation. You have to be the one to decide. I am not
going to tell you what to do."

She looked around the kitchen, hating that he saw
things so clearly. She couldn't fake her way through with
Clay. And yet admitting the truth seemed so impossible.

He came over to her and knelt by the table. "What is
it?"

"I'm scared."

"Scared of what?" He put his wide, warm palm on her
thigh, a friendly gesture but one that scored her heart just
the same because she wished it came from a different sort
of sentiment.

"Of everything. Of living, of dying, of failing. Just
because I know you were right today doesn't mean I can

snap my fingers and just fix how I feel. You told me weeks ago that I could either quit, go through it or around it. I've been trying to go around it all, Clay, and it's not working. I don't want to quit. And going through it is *hard.*"

"But you're forgetting something," he said firmly, giving her knee a squeeze. "You don't have to go through it alone."

In her heart of hearts, Meg wished he meant something different than what he did. But she wasn't stupid. She didn't read anything into the words that wasn't there.

"Talk to your mom and dad. Dawson. Your friends. Like I said, no one expects you to be perfect. You're human. You went away to protect everyone but you don't need to. Let them in."

"Like you do?"

He bounced on his toes a few times and treated her to a wry smile. "Men don't talk about feelings the same way."

"You're telling me."

Clay patted her knee and stood up. "This is a community, Meg. Yes, there are gossips and busybodies, but there's also a helping hand and understanding when you need it. People will want you to succeed. That's what we do when one of our own is in need."

"Damn you," she said, but then she laughed, disbelieving but somehow very, very relieved now that the words were out and not pressing on her lungs. She pressed her hands to her warm cheeks. "I should say no. Money and friends rarely turns out well..."

"I can draw up terms if you'd like. Have Brianna Johnson look after it."

"I'll want the payment schedule in writing," she insisted, but the fizz of excitement built again. She was so close to getting what she wanted.

"Done."

He held out his right hand, waiting for her to shake. One eyebrow arched up as he paused. "Gentlemen's agreement until it's put to paper." he nudged her.

Gentlemen's agreement. A handshake of equals. Meg's chest swelled with the gesture. "Agreed," she said, before she could change her mind. She put her hand in his, feeling his fingers close around hers. He held it a little too long as their gazes caught. The kitchen was completely, utterly silent. He had to do something soon before she was tempted to make a fool of herself.

But where would it lead? Nothing had changed. She was still the same. Still scarred. Still afraid. And so was Clay. She pulled her hand out of his.

"About the other night," she said quietly.

"It won't happen again," he replied firmly. "We just got carried away. Maybe Aunt Stacy was right about weddings after all."

It was the assurance she wanted but it left her feeling strangely empty.

But now her idea was on the cusp of becoming a reality and she couldn't stop the anticipation that began to take hold. "This is really going to happen."

"You bet your boots," Clay announced, and clapped his hands together, seemingly unaffected. "Now, call Linda and tell her you won't be home for dinner. I'll take out another steak and you can tell me your plans."

CHAPTER EIGHT

BRIANNA JOHNSON'S office was a study of organization and precision. She had the papers in order, pens at the ready, and before Meg could catch her breath it was all done. All that was left was transferring the money to Meg's new business account.

Meg looked up at Clay, feeling slightly sick. There was no taking it back now. The enormity of the job ahead sank in as well as the knowledge that for years to come, she was linked to Clay Gregory.

He smiled down at her, his dark eyes crinkling at the corners. "Let's go celebrate."

Celebrate? Meg thought maybe she should just sit down for a moment since her feet seemed to be feeling slightly numb. Maybe it was an extremities thing because she felt a little light-headed, too. She hadn't eaten breakfast, she realized, having been too keyed up about this morning's meeting. Now it was nearly lunch.

"Okay," she answered, gripping the strap of her purse. "Where to?"

"You choose."

"How about the Inn?" They were both dressed up for the appointment—or at least, out of ranch gear, and their clothing would be totally appropriate for the Inn's dining room. Meg had worn dark trousers and a drop-sleeve cashmere sweater in gray that she'd received last Christmas, and Clay had left his denims in the closet, going business casual. Her mouth watered at more than the thought of lunch. Why shouldn't they make an occasion of it? Today was the start of something very exciting.

At Clay's surprised expression Meg felt heat rush down her body. Of course. The Inn was quiet, but it was also the most intimate of all the locations in town with lots of private corners and alcoves. Meg hurried to explain. "There's not an abundance of options," she remarked. "It's quieter there and I want to get your opinion about a few things."

He lifted an eyebrow. "I thought the deal was that I was strictly hands-off. No butting my nose in."

"It's not butting your nose in if I ask for your input," she replied loftily. "Of course if you'd rather not…"

"I didn't say that." He shifted his weight on to one hip. "I just want to clarify things before I go breaking any of your rules."

Rules. He was standing there in black cotton pants and a light blue shirt that showed off a tan he'd already started building from working outside. She could think of a few rules she wouldn't mind him breaking. *Not a good idea*, she reminded herself. She would be completely over her head. But it didn't take away the fact that the breaking of them would be very, very fun.

"The rules are safe for today." Meg straightened her shoulders. "So are we on?"

"The Inn it is," Clay agreed, holding out a hand to let her go first. Meg held on to the banister going down the stairs. She was still feeling a bit woozy but lifted her head, determined Clay not see anything amiss. She'd just signed the papers, the last thing she needed was him clucking around like some mother hen. She was hungry, that was all.

They walked the block and a half to the Inn and found themselves the sole occupants of the dining room as the lunch rush—such as it could be called in Larch Valley—hadn't yet begun. They were seated in a back corner, more private than Meg was comfortable with, but she straightened her shoulders. She could do this. She'd put aside her feelings for Clay for a long time and they'd remained friends. It didn't have to be different now. She valued his opinion, and now that things were settled she was anxious to move forward. She just needed to keep things businesslike.

She grabbed her bag and reached for her folder of plans when Clay's hand stopped her. "Take a few minutes to celebrate," he said softly. "Don't you want to look at your menu?"

"I don't need to," she answered with a tight smile. "The cream of vegetable soup is fantastic."

She put the folder on the table. "I wanted you to see the plans and tell me what you think."

"Plans?" He wrinkled his brow. "You have plans drawn up? Already?"

"Of course."

Clay's brow puckered. "How long have you had them?"

"I had them drawn up last fall." Meg held out the papers. She'd convinced Dawson to hook her up with a builder, and she knew he'd thought she'd forget any schemes once she was well again. He'd been wrong.

"But you were still in Calgary."

"I was doing chemo, Clay. I'd lost my hair and spent a lot of the time with my head in the toilet. I needed something to look forward to. A reason to keep going. I think the family thought I'd let it go once I was well. But the more time passed, the more I was certain." Today Meg was feeling like life was finally spread out in front of her and that it just might be okay to open up a little about what her treatment had been like. "I've been feeling so much better lately, and my last checkup was perfect. Now I already have a head start."

He held out his hand for the plans just as the waitress came to take their order. After she was gone, Clay moved a seat over and spread them out on the tabletop.

Meg looked at the drawings sideways and felt excitement and nerves fizz through her veins. In addition to their current stable, an extension was planned to the east side to accommodate another ten stalls. The current corral was shifted to a more central position, with access to it from both the stable and through a sliding door along the new indoor ring. To the west side of the ring was a planned outdoor ring and across the extended driveway was a garden, complete with a large perennial bed and X's he saw were meant to be picnic tables.

"You're sure ten stalls is enough?"

"We've got ten already, and we're only using four. The plan is to purchase a half dozen good horses to use for general lessons or trail rides and leave the last ten for boarders."

"You really have thought it through."

"I had a lot of time to think. But you're surprised."

He shook his head. "Not at all. I wouldn't have loaned you the money if I didn't think you had your i's dotted and your t's crossed."

"When did you start having so much faith in me?" she asked, watching him fold up the papers. It was a charged question but one she really wanted the answer to.

"I always have," he replied, handing the sheets back to her. For a second they each held a corner until he let go. "Maybe that's why it bothered me so much when you went away for treatment. I had never seen you run from anything. I'd never seen you turn your back on…people you cared about. But I don't think I understood how scared you were."

Their food came and Meg watched as Clay dipped a sweet potato fry in aioli sauce and bit into it, then licked the remnants from his lip. She swallowed. Felt a familiar tingling of awareness on one side of her body. Clay turned her on. There was no two ways around it. And no way around the fact that she was still too afraid to act on it, especially since he made it clear that the night in her foyer had been a one-time occurrence. She wasn't into playing games or sending mixed signals, so she grabbed her spoon and dipped into the fragrant soup.

"Meg?"

"Hmm?"

He wiped his hands on a napkin. "Will you let me help? Not because I'm protecting an investment. But because I want to? I think you're going to do something special and exciting and I'd like to be involved."

"You mean I'd get to be your boss?"

A grin flirted with his cheek. "You're in command."

Meg didn't know what to say. She put down her spoon and drew in a breath. Being in command of Clay Gregory was heady business. Certainly throngs of women would love to hear those words from his lips and she wasn't immune, either. But he didn't mean it that way and she knew it. And she didn't want his interference. Being near him was becoming more difficult with every passing day.

"I look at the plans and I look at you and it clicks, Meg." He pushed his case. "I can see it in my head."

She could, too. She wished she and Clay weren't on

the same wavelength quite so often. It made keeping him at arm's length very difficult.

She had to keep things strictly business. "I was thinking of the Lund Brothers for construction, what do you think?"

"They'd do a good job for you. Good honest work and they won't spend a dime they don't have to. Plus they have good subcontractors."

Meg pushed her empty bowl away. "That's what I was thinking, too."

She knew she hadn't answered his question. She hoped he'd forget about it and not push the matter. She wasn't quite sure how she felt about it. It would be sweet torture having him around all the time.

But it wouldn't be all the time, she reasoned as she stood and reached for her wallet. Clay had a ranch to run. He'd made the offer but she doubted he'd have the time to truly make good on it. Maybe his intentions were good, but how much would he really be around?

"I've got this." He put his hand over hers. Her fingers clutched the wallet, half in and half out of her bag. He was standing beside her, too close, the remnants of his sandwich left on his plate. His fingers tightened around her wrist and Meg's heart kicked into overdrive. If she stood up all the way she'd nearly be pressed into his body. But she couldn't stay stooped over forever.

He gave a tug on her wrist and she stood. The corner concealed them from the smattering of diners who had wandered in over the last few minutes and the air caught in her lungs, making her breaths painfully short.

His gaze plumbed hers for several seconds and she couldn't make herself pull away.

He was waiting. Encouraging, certainly, and not backing off. But he was also leaving the choice in her hands.

She leaned forward the tiniest bit. His lips were right there, full, luscious, waiting to be kissed. His body grazed hers, making the cashmere of her sweater slide across her skin. Oh, heavens…

Meg leaned forward another half inch, and Clay's tongue slipped out to wet his lips.

She dropped her wallet.

It hit on the edge of the table on the way down, upending a bundle of cutlery and sending it clattering to the floor. Meg stumbled a step backward as the half dozen people in the dining room raised their heads at the sound.

She couldn't look at him. Instead she knelt to the floor to pick up the flatware, cheeks blazing.

"Oh, miss, don't worry about it." The waitress hurried over and reassured her with a smile. "I've got this."

Meg's only option was to stand up and face Clay. Face them all. She rose slowly, picking up her wallet and tucking it into her purse. Finally, torturously, she met Clay's gaze. He'd taken out his wallet and placed enough cash on the table to cover their bill and a sizable tip.

The waitress left them alone and Meg searched for something to say.

"Not quite as over as we thought, then," Clay murmured, his deep voice riding over her already raw nerve endings.

"Clay…" Her body shivered at the implication. It had to be over. They couldn't keep going on this way.

"You're in charge," he reminded her, but she no longer knew if he meant about them or about the ranch or if there was really any difference. And she didn't want to be in charge of their relationship. It was different than the black and white of business. Being in charge meant being responsible for screwing up. It was easier blaming someone else.

"I'm in charge," she echoed quietly.

He smiled then, his whole face lighting up while his eyes seemed to tempt and tease. "Come on, Squirt. I'll walk you to your car."

It should have bothered her. She should say something. But instead all she felt was a warmth spreading through her at the affection she heard in the nickname.

She shouldn't get used to relying on Clay. But as they left the Inn and he walked her back to her car, she knew it was too late. She relied on him for so many things she needed, and she couldn't help feeling like at some point it was all going to end in a huge thud.

Meg slid the drill back into her tool belt and straightened, stretching out her back. Lord, but she was tired today. She didn't know what was wrong with her. She'd slept like the dead last night; there was no reason for her to be dragging her butt around today. She coughed and rolled her shoulders.

While the Lund Brothers took a coffee break, she finished screwing one of the two-by-fours to a fence post in the new outdoor ring. Once the fence was done, she'd set to work building the picnic tables for the garden area. The supplies waited in a neat pile under a tarp. As Clay's truck turned up the driveway in a cloud of dust, Meg reached for another board, measured, measured again to be sure, and went to the sawhorse. The circular saw trimmed the end off in no time and by the time he was hopping out of the cab she had the board carefully lined up and had put in the first long screw. She pressed her hand to her forehead. The headache from this morning wasn't going away. But there was work to be done, and no headache or sexy rancher was going to keep her from getting it completed.

"It's really coming along." Clay's voice sounded behind her and she felt the rush of heat that always followed when he spoke in that warm, approving tone.

"Now that the framing is done, things will start moving fairly quickly," Meg replied, sinking the last screw in the board and turning. She spun rather too quickly and it felt like the earth shifted beneath her feet for just a moment. It righted again soon after and she forced a smile.

"What's wrong?"

"Nothing," she replied quickly. "What are you doing here?"

"I'm on my way into town, and wanted to know if you needed anything. And to see how things are progressing." He smiled at her. "But it looks like you have everything under control."

Meg went to the box containing the screws and refilled her pouch. "The fence design was a good idea. I like it a lot."

"If you wait until after supper, I can help you. The days are longer and we'll have the light."

The idea of working side by side with Clay was tempting, but that was the problem. He was far too tempting and she could still hear his husky voice in the restaurant saying they were not as over as they'd thought. No matter how she turned it over in her head the facts spoke for themselves. She always came up against the same thing. She couldn't ever imagine revealing herself—all of herself—to Clay. And Clay wasn't the committing kind, especially not with her. To her recollection she'd never seen him date a girl longer than a month at the outside. It would be too great a chance, playing the odds.

"That's okay," she answered, taking a moment to lean against the sawhorse and catch her breath. "I'll have this section done tonight and that only leaves one more. I'll be able to start on the tables after that."

"You're sure?"

"Positive. You must have stuff to do."

He looked down at her waist and let his gaze do a slow travel up her body, raising her temperature a few notches. When it settled on her face his lips held a sexy, teasing twist and his eyes glittered at her. "Nothing that looks as good as you in that tool belt."

"Clay." She had to stop that sort of talk right now. Not because it was inappropriate but because it gave her ideas.

"I'm just teasing," he replied, but he hooked his thumbs in his pockets. "Sorta. I admire a capable woman who knows her way around power tools."

"What I'm doing is sending you on your way," she countered. She put her hand on her face. Goodness, was that heat from her blush in her cheeks? The May morning wasn't quite *that* hot. She gave a shiver. Actually it wasn't very hot at all.

"Meg, are you all right?"

"Of course, why shouldn't I be?"

"You looked funny again."

Meg picked up a one-by-six and pulled out her measuring tape. She wasn't feeling one hundred percent, but she was just tired. Since breaking ground she'd been pulling a lot of late nights. "Buzz off, Clay," she said lightly. "Just what a girl wants to hear. That she looks funny."

She measured and marked the board and took it to the sawhorse. Laid it across and reached for the circular saw. But then, very carefully, she put the saw down. Something wasn't right. And using a power saw was probably not a good choice at this moment.

"I nearly forgot, I told Mom I'd send her with an errand list before she went to work." She threw the words out quickly to cover her pause and straightened.

Clay looked into Meg's face. She was not all right, no matter what she said. Her eyes were glassy and her face was as white as a sheet.

"Megan."

She began to weave and Clay felt his heart drop to his toes. She stared at him blindly. "Megan," he insisted, stepping forward.

She started the slow slide and he moved in to catch her. Meg was a slight girl but the force of her dead weight caught him by surprise. Every worry he'd held on to for the past year seemed to center in his gut as he slid his arm beneath her legs and picked her up, tools and all.

As he crossed the farmyard, only one question seemed burned on his brain: Was her cancer back?

It sounded dramatic but it wasn't such a leap, considering what she'd been through. He hadn't been there to see her illness the first time around and the idea of it nearly frightened him out of his boots. Nothing could happen to Meg. He wouldn't let it. If she thought she could push everyone away this time she could think again.

Halfway to the house she stirred in his arms. Thank God. Her eyelids were fluttering and he could feel the heat of her against his sleeves. She was too hot.

"Put me down," she insisted weakly, but Clay ignored her.

"Put me down," she repeated, and this time Clay spared her a glance.

"Not a chance," he ground out, his strides long and purposeful. Linda saw them coming and was on the front step, holding the door open.

"What happened?"

Linda's face was ashen as she shut the door behind

them and followed on Clay's footsteps. Clay carried Meg straight through to the living room, still in his boots, and laid her on the sofa. For a breath of a moment his face changed, softened, and his hand grazed her cheek. Then her mother bustled in and the moment was lost.

Meg bit down on her lip. Clay had placed her so gently on the sofa she wanted to cry. Why couldn't he be like this all the time? Why did it take such worry and fear to bring out this tender side of him? She blinked slowly and looked up into their faces. "Stop it," she said loudly, so loudly it was startling in the quiet room. "Stop looking at me that way. I'm not dying."

They both had the grace to look guilty at least. Meg moved to push herself up and Clay stepped in. She'd never seen his face so determined. So...her heart sank. Worried. Afraid. Not that he wanted her to see it. But she'd known him long enough to know when he was freaking out on the inside and the wild look in his eyes and stubborn set to his jaw told the tale. "Oh, no, you don't," he commanded. "I'm not catching you again."

He'd caught her? Meg wanted to drop through the floor. Swooning like some...well, she didn't know what. She had no experience with fainting. She felt like such a goose.

Linda put her hand to Meg's forehead. "Lord, you're burning up. I'm going for the thermometer."

She hurried out of the room leaving Meg alone with Clay. "You can go now." Meg mustered up her most dismissive voice. Clay only laughed. Harshly.

"You're in no position to dismiss me," he answered, and sat beside her on the sofa. He, too, pressed his hand to her face. His palm felt cool and lovely and she was reminded of how he'd cupped her jaw in his fingers before kissing her.

"Like an angel," she murmured, leaning into his palm.

"You're feverish," he said, withdrawing his hand. "What do you think you were doing?"

"I'm not feverish," she defended. Except she knew that she was. Angels? Did she really say that? She had to be delirious. "It's nothing. I'm just a little tired. I've been staying up late."

"People don't faint from a few late nights," Clay retorted. Linda returned with an old thermometer and popped it in Meg's mouth.

"I don't need…" The words came out muffled around the thermometer.

"Be quiet and keep that under your tongue," her mother ordered.

They were treating her like a child. Meg's eyes burned with humiliation. She'd rather be passed out in a lump in the farmyard than treated this way. She pulled the thermometer out of her mouth and waved it in the air. "I forgot to eat this morning, okay?"

Clay neatly snagged the thermometer and shoved it back in her mouth. She glared at him.

"Skipping breakfast. Late nights. Working impossibly long days. You're doing a great job looking after yourself, aren't you?"

He had a point, not that she'd let him know it. She moved to protest and he held up a finger. "Leave that in your mouth. Or I'll make you, and you know I can do it."

If the fever hadn't flushed her cheeks, the embarrassment from that did. She pretended she was shooting daggers at him with her eyes. If he'd just leave, she'd make a cup of tea and have some toast and maybe sleep for an hour to two and be right as rain again.

Linda took the thermometer and read it while Meg pouted. "I'll take a nap and have something to eat, okay? There's no need for this fuss."

"One hundred and two," Linda reported. Meg heard the quiver in her voice and closed her eyes. This was why she'd gone to Calgary. Every fever, every light-headed, nauseous moment would have had Linda in a flutter. She didn't want to worry any of them. "I'm fine," she insisted.

"I'm taking you to the doctor," Clay announced. "Right now."

"I'll get her purse. You'll want her medical card."

"You're both overreacting."

"Indulge me." Clay watched Linda leave the room and leaned forward. "Indulge your mother," he murmured. "She's worried. Put her mind at ease."

"It's just a bit of a fever."

Clay raised one eyebrow.

Meg didn't have the energy to fight. With each passing moment she was feeling more wretched. They wouldn't believe her if she said a simple bug would cause her no lasting harm.

"Fine," she acquiesced with a burdensome sigh. "Could I have some water before we go? I'm thirsty."

"I'll be right back."

Clay went to the kitchen. Meg heard the tap running and heard her mother's voice, followed by Clay's lower one. Her joints were starting to ache as she pushed herself to a sitting position and unhooked the tool belt. When she went to pull it out from behind her back, a twinge ran from her armpit down her arm. Instinctively her hand went to the flat wall of her chest where her breast used to be.

She bit down on her lip, yanked on the belt and left it in a heap on the sofa.

She would not borrow trouble. Would not let her life be governed by fear like Clay, like her mother.

She would not.

CHAPTER NINE

MEG huddled under the hospital blanket and shivered. What she wanted was a cup of hot tea and to go home to bed.

There was nothing to worry about. And yet she was worried. She'd learned long ago that keeping information from doctors never solved anything, so during her examination she mentioned the twinges she'd been feeling. She'd been thoroughly examined and blood drawn. Now she was stuck here waiting for the results.

"I brought you some tea." Clay pushed the curtain aside and came to the bed. She pushed herself to sitting and reached for the cup. The acetaminophen she'd been given was helping, though she didn't trust herself to get up. She took a sip of the hot tea and it tasted wonderful.

"I can't believe they let you in here." The emergency room wasn't exactly private and she kept her voice low. Curtains separated one bed from the next. Clay looked at the bed, but seemed to reconsider and sat on the chair where Meg's purse and coat were draped.

"It was taking a long time and I was pacing. I might have…stretched the truth a little."

She lifted her brows in a silent question.

"I mentioned your medical history and I might have said that I was your boyfriend."

Meg took another sip of tea so he couldn't see her face. Boyfriend? Clay? He'd acted like one today, but things were certainly not to that level nor would they ever be. She wanted to believe he was here for support but she knew there was a whole lot of fear at play.

"And Mom?"

"She went to work. I told her I'd call her the moment we heard anything."

Once more Clay was stepping in to help. Why did he always seem to be in the right place at the right time? She wanted to resent him for it but couldn't. He was here, which meant nothing at home was disrupted.

"Clay...thank you. For bringing me in and waiting. I know you have things to do."

"Don't worry about that. They'll keep. How are you feeling? You look awful."

She heard the worry in his voice. She could never tell him about the odd twinges that came and went or the tightness she'd felt in her arm lately. "I'm sure it's just the flu," she said, leaning back on the pillows. "The pain relievers are helping the fever, I think, and I'm a bit achy."

"What did the doctor say?"

"He did an exam and they drew some blood. That's what we're waiting for. But, Clay, I just had my latest checkup two weeks ago and everything was clear. There's no need to worry."

"I'll wait to hear it from the doctor," Clay replied, sitting back in the chair.

Meg drank a bit more tea and then handed it back, knowing it was pointless to argue with him. "You do that. I'm tired."

She must have been exhausted because she fell asleep instantly and only woke again when the doctor came through the curtain. She rubbed her eyes and sighed.

Her body felt like it had been hit by a truck. Whatever was going on in there, it had knocked her flat.

"Well, Megan, you were right. It does look like a simple but nasty flu bug. Doesn't hurt to be cautious in your case, though. Stay in bed, take acetaminophen for the fever and in a couple of days you'll feel fine."

"Thanks, Doc." She looked at Clay. The strained look around his eyes had eased. "I told you it was nothing," she said as smugly as she could muster.

The doctor laughed. "Can't blame a man for worrying about you," he said kindly. "But you can put your mind at ease." He smiled at Clay and then shifted his gaze back to Meg.

"The twinges you've been feeling aren't uncommon, by the way, and you mentioned they only happen when you're doing physical labor, so I'm going to suggest a massage therapist who specializes in this sort of thing. Releasing some of the tension and tightness should help. But what I did notice was the swelling in your right arm. Did your doctor in Calgary talk to you about edema?"

She wished Clay wasn't sitting beside her, listening to every word. She hadn't told anyone other than her doctors about the occasional tightening she felt. Now edema?

She was used to the talk of side effects and all the strange things that happened to the body during and after cancer treatment. But Clay wasn't, and the effect was obvious on his face. He'd blow it all out of proportion. "A bit," she replied, adding honestly, "but a long time ago. After my surgery."

"It can take a while to show up post-op. And it's common as well, especially after removal of lymph nodes or radiation. I'm going to refer you to a clinic. In the meantime, I want you to wear gloves while you're working to protect from scratches and cuts. We don't want you getting an infection. Keeping the arm moving and elevating it can help, too."

"Thanks, Doc."

"You're doing fantastic, Megan." He patted her knee. "Sometimes it takes a while for things to resolve, that's all. Take the next few days to rest and get some well-earned sleep."

"She will. I'll make sure of it," Clay said, and Meg gritted her teeth. Oh, this was just the ammo he needed, wasn't it? If he'd stayed in the waiting room she could have walked out, announced it was the flu and that would have been the end of it. But he had to come in with tea and it had been so nice to have him with her rather than sitting all alone like she was used to. She'd relaxed and fallen asleep and there hadn't been time—and she hadn't had the presence of mind—to ask him to leave during the talk with the doctor.

The doctor swept out of the curtained area and Clay reached for her coat. "Come on, let's get you home and into bed."

It had a hollow ring to it and Meg took a few breaths to gather herself. She would say thank-you because despite his heavy-handedness he was trying to help. She would not pick a fight. She had to pick her battles and today she didn't have the energy to win. "I'll call Mom from the truck," she said, and then looked pointedly at Clay. "You can wait outside, Clay. I need to change."

For the first time he seemed to notice her jeans and shirt folded neatly on the side table. He blushed. Meg was sick but she took pleasure in the fact that she'd managed to shake his implacable control.

"Do you want me to get a nurse? What if you faint again?"

He was going to suffocate her if she didn't get some

space soon. "I'm feeling a little better since the medicine. Truly. Give me five minutes."

He slid out of the curtained area and Meg leaned back against the pillows. His worry was pressing down on her, but there was also a little spot inside that felt empty now that he was gone. Anytime that little hole of loneliness had shown up in Calgary, she'd pulled up her socks and reminded herself that she was sparing her family concern and worry.

But she could only maintain that for so long, and she'd been home long enough now that she'd let down her guard. She was tired of being alone. She wanted to share things with someone. She knew Clay wanted to be there for her but the problem was he couldn't be there all the way. She wished they were close enough that he could have gently helped her with her clothes. That he might have held her hand while the doctor was talking. Or that they'd talk about it afterward, not from fear, but from sharing.

But Clay didn't want to share. He wanted to do. He looked at it as a step-by-step road map to getting better with no deviations, no exceptions. And it wasn't that simple. It would never be that simple. There were too many uncertainties.

Meg carefully slid off the bed and slowly dressed, leaving the hospital gown on the mussed sheets. She ripped the tape and cotton ball from her arm; she could still see the needle hole from her blood work. Truth was, she felt wretched and trying to sort this out today was an exercise in futility.

Clay was waiting by the sliding doors when she went through. Without asking, he put his arm around her waist. She tolerated it because she knew protesting was useless.

In no time at all they were back on the road, heading to Larch Valley and the Briggs ranch.

They were nearly at the turnoff when Clay finally spoke.

"You're finished working on the expansion."

Meg had the flu, she was feverish and felt like she'd been dragged through a knothole, but Clay's don't-give-me-any-arguments tone put her back up. She straightened in her seat. "I beg your pardon?"

"It's too much, too hard on you. You're wearing yourself out."

The laugh that came from Meg's throat sounded like it belonged to someone else. "I must be delirious, because it sounded like you just forbade me to do something."

Clay pulled over to the side of the road and shoved the truck into Park so fiercely that Meg paused. She'd never seen him like this before, so hard and uncompromising, unable to be cajoled out of his grumpiness. This was different and she waited for the outburst that was surely coming.

He let the truck idle but turned in his seat. "What is it going to take, Meg? When are you going to stop this ridiculous idea that you have to be and do everything yourself?" He pointed a finger at her. "The doctor said rest, and by God that's what you're going to do."

"I have the flu!" she yelled back at him. "Just. The. Flu. I am not dying. The cancer is not back. So back off, Clay. Back right off."

"You never told me about the twinges. About any swelling."

Meg made a dismissive sound in her throat. "Because I knew this would happen. You should have waited in the waiting room. I could have handled this just fine."

"Right. Because you're a pro at handling things, aren't you? You never let anyone in."

"Look, I have enough to do dealing with my own feelings and thoughts, never mind your neuroses." She gave a harsh laugh. "Me not let anyone in? That's rich coming from *you*."

"Neuroses?" There was a pause of shocked silence before he continued, his voice low with warning. "You're done. No more heavy lifting or fence building or any of that stuff, you hear?"

"I most certainly do not." Good heavens, yes, she was tired but nothing that would warrant this dramatic reaction. She looked at Clay and fought to be rational rather than reactive. "I know what you heard today scared you, Clay. But, really, it's no big deal. It is all part of the recovery and stuff I knew I might have to deal with. So let's just leave it. I want to go home and get to bed. Because contrary to popular belief, I do have some sense in my head. And when I'm feeling better, I will be back to work and there's not a damn thing you can do about it."

"I can recall the loan."

Meg paled even more than she already was. He wouldn't. He...couldn't. She scrambled to put thoughts together. "We signed an agreement. You can't just pull funding because you want to." Never was she so glad that she'd insisted on an official arrangement.

"I'll find a way around it. It's for your own good."

"What happened to believing in me? Trusting me?"

Clay gripped the steering wheel with both hands. "This has nothing to do with that."

But Meg disagreed. "It has *everything* to do with that. Do you think I'm stupid? That I don't know my own limitations? That I don't worry? What should I do, Clay? Stop living for the next forty years? I don't work that way. Love isn't wrapping someone up in bubble wrap and getting them to the end unscathed!"

"Love? Who said anything about love?"

The words rang through the cab of the truck. She could have blamed it on the flu or the need for more meds, but she would be a liar. The bottomless feeling she was experiencing right now had nothing to do with being sick. Of course Clay didn't love her. He never had, not the way she wanted. He wanted someone he could control and order about. He wanted promises and guarantees. She could offer him none of those things.

"Take me home," she said into the charged silence. Clay opened his mouth but she held up a hand. "No. Please, don't say anything more. I don't have the energy to argue with you anymore today, Clay. Take me home and leave me alone."

Wordlessly he put the truck in gear and pulled back out on to the road. A few minutes later they were home. Meg got out of the truck and didn't even look up at him. She just shut the door and walked to the house. After she was inside she heard the roar of his truck as he spun out the driveway.

She went straight to her room and under the covers, shivering with fever and fighting tears. After several minutes her swollen lids grew heavy and just before dropping off to sleep she realized she hadn't called her mother.

She sat up to reach for the phone and snuffled. She couldn't call like this. Instead she picked up her cell and sent a quick text message. Then she turned off the ringer.

If anyone wanted more than that from her today, they were simply going to have to deal with the disappointment.

Clay slammed the door of his truck and stomped to the house. He took perverse pleasure in slamming the front door as well and then stood in the middle of the hall, wondering what the heck he was supposed to do next.

He let out a great breath and dropped his head.

He was an idiot. A real jerk. Meg was sick and all he'd done was throw ultimatums around and yell at her because he'd been absolutely terrified.

Because despite his best intentions, he'd gone and fallen in love with her. He'd known it the moment she'd collapsed in his arms and his heart had frozen with fear. Damn it. What a mess.

"Serves her right," he muttered. "Scaring me like that."

"Serves who right?"

Clay nearly jumped out of his skin. Stacy came around the corner of the kitchen, leaned against the doorway and gave him her trademark visual examination, just as she had when he'd been a boy and she'd ruled the ranch.

"What are you doing here?"

"That's a fine way to welcome your auntie," she chided, pushing away from the doorjamb and grinning. "Slamming doors and muttering to yourself. My, you are in a state. What's Megan done now?"

Clay realized his mouth had been hanging open and he shut it. He stared at Stacy and frowned. "Who said anything about Megan?"

Stacy laughed, came forward and patted his arm. "You could frighten small children with that scowl, Clay. And I know it's Megan because no woman can put that dark look on your face like she can."

"She hasn't done anything." The anger that had felt justified drained away after he said it. Megan hadn't done anything, it was him. All him. He knew it and didn't like it. He met Stacy's gaze. "And Megan does not put a 'dark look' on my face, as you say."

Stacy's smile slid away. "Yes, she does. I came to pick

up a few things I left behind, but they can wait. Mike is picking me up later, so let's go talk. You clearly need to."

He had work to do. He had a thousand excuses he could give her, but he knew she'd see through each and every one. She always did. Stacy knew him better than anyone else. She'd been through it all with him.

They went out on to the back porch. Stacy handed him a bottle of beer and twisted off the top of her own. "Sit," she said, and he knew it wasn't a suggestion. He could have put up a stink about being a grown man and so on. But Stacy was, for all intents and purposes, his mother. And she'd brought him up better than that. So he sat, twisted off the top of his beer, took a drink and sighed.

Stacy simply waited.

Clay closed his eyes and let the spring sun soak into his face. "Meg's sick."

"Oh, Clay…"

"Not that sick. The flu. But, like you, I jumped to conclusions. I possibly overreacted."

"Possibly?"

He couldn't help the chuckle that erupted from her dry, knowing question.

"I yelled at her. I issued ultimatums. I was a jerk."

"Because?"

This was the hard part. He knew what the problem was deep down but admitting it was something else entirely. "Because the thought of her being sick again scares me to death. And because if she were sick again, I'd want to be there for her. And that's crazy, right? To put myself through something like that knowing what might happen."

"And you lashed out, right?" When he didn't answer, Stacy sighed. "Oh, Clay, you always had a way of shutting out those people who could hurt you most. Your dad. Your mom. Meg."

"Not you."

"Because you trusted me. It wasn't easy stepping in, you know. I knew if I ever let you down you'd close the door on me like you did them. Don't think it didn't cause me some sleepless nights, because it did. Especially in your teenage years. What did you say to Meg?"

"I told her she couldn't work on the expansion anymore. Threatened to call in the loan."

"Clay Gregory!" Her bottle hit the patio table with a *thunk*.

"I know," he groaned, leaning forward and resting his elbows on his knees. "She made me so mad, Stace. Here I was worried sick about her and she's…"

"She's what, Clay? Living?"

He swallowed.

"I didn't say I was right," he added, taking a long pull of the beer. He swallowed and admitted, "She just knows what buttons to push."

"Do you love her?"

She drove him crazy. She made him angry and made him laugh and the way she kissed set his blood on fire. If he left all the complications out of the equation, if he could manage to forget the issue of her mortality for just a moment he knew the answer. "I do." He uttered a soft curse. "And it's wrong, all wrong."

"Because of her cancer?"

"Not just that." He remembered watching his father withering away. Remembered waking up and realizing his mother was gone. "Cancer's only part of it. I know that now. I'm so afraid of letting myself love her and then losing her."

"Oh, Clay." Stacy's voice thickened with emotion. "I'm

sorry you're hurting, honey, but I'm also so very glad. I was worried you wouldn't ever let yourself love anyone."

A breeze fluttered across the porch, ruffling the newly sprouted poplar leaves on the shade tree. The truth was sitting right there in front of him. He could admit it. What he didn't know was what to do about it.

"I can't stop how I feel. Or how I worry. If I can't imagine life without her now, how much worse would it be if…"

"I know," Stacy said simply.

Clay felt marginally better letting the feelings out. Not that a damn thing was solved, but things had been such a mess in his head and voicing it had helped.

"I got lucky the day I got you," he said, looking over at her. She looked happy. She was nearing fifty but there was a sparkle in her eye that had been missing for too long and it had been reconnecting with Mike that had put it there. Clay had been afraid to care for someone too deeply for a long time. But lately he'd felt like something was missing. The only time things had clicked into place was when he was with Meg.

"You were the son I never had," she replied, and smiled. "We've been in this together for a long time. Just be patient, Clay. Meg's been through a lot. And she needs you, whether she's willing to admit it or not. I saw her idolize you when you were kids. I saw you at the wedding dance. Don't give up. On her or on yourself. You are not your mother. You're made of much sterner stuff, I promise you."

He already knew he was. Meg wasn't getting rid of him that easily. And he wasn't giving up. That wasn't the hard part. It was acceptance and letting go. Knowing that he really had no say in how all this played out. If he pursued something with Meg—something real—it meant acknowledging that there were no guarantees. Willingly putting himself out there, knowing what might happen. Doing exactly what he'd promised himself he'd never, ever do.

"I owe her an apology," he said quietly, putting his empty bottle on the table.

"I'm sure you do." When he looked askance at his aunt she wore an impish expression. "You were probably a real idiot."

He shrugged, the only confirmation she was going to get, but a ghost of a smile tipped his lips. "I won't be delivering it today. Today she's in bed resting."

"Well, she's probably mad, too. A few days to cool down isn't necessarily a bad thing."

They were sitting companionably in the afternoon silence when they heard a tap of a horn. "Mike," Stacy said with a smile, putting her hands on the arms of her chair and pushing herself up to standing. "I'd better get going."

"Aunt Stacy?"

He didn't often put the aunt in front of her name and when he did it was usually because he was being particularly serious. And he was. He hadn't told her how grateful he was very often.

He got up and went to her, folding her into a hug. "I love you," he murmured, then let her go.

"And I love you." She blinked several times and her smile wobbled just a bit. "You need anything—want to talk—you give a holler, okay?"

But Clay knew what he had to do, and he had to do it on his own. There were things to be faced that Stacy didn't understand. It wasn't just him standing in their way.

Meg might be determined to make a go of her project, but one thing still paralyzed her. And that was the idea of anyone seeing the evidence of her mastectomy. Maybe he'd finally accepted the depth of his feelings for her, but Meg had a long way to go before she trusted him to stick. He couldn't blame her. He'd given her so many reasons to doubt him.

Maybe there were ways around roadblocks, and Clay considered himself a smart man, but he really had no idea how to solve that problem.

CHAPTER TEN

MEG stayed in bed the better part of two days. The fever broke and she felt immeasurably better, but exhausted. Linda fed her soup and toast and brought movies home from the video store. The two of them curled up in front of the television in the evening, Meg snuggled in a blanket and they watched chick flicks. Months ago she would have felt suffocated by the constant attention. But things had changed. She'd loosened up a little, and she could see beyond herself enough now to realize that her mom was only doing what good moms did. Trying to look after her kid.

She waited for Clay to call, but he didn't. On the third day she showered and dressed and went out to see what was happening with the barn. In just the few days she'd been off the scene the trusses were up and the roof finished. Lord, it was going up so fast, she thought, letting some of the old excitement revive her. There was so much more to do on the business front, too—business cards to order, advertising, setting up a website and registration for classes. She remembered a few weeks ago Clay had suggested she hold a grand opening to kick it all off. She'd loved the suggestion at the time and they'd thrown around some ideas, but nothing seemed the same now without him and the idea of a party had lost its luster.

They'd had words in the past but this time had felt so final. Even last year, when he'd told her exactly what he thought about her going away for treatment, it had still felt like a door was left open, just a bit. But not this time and Meg felt his absence keenly. From the beginning he'd been the one to support her venture, first in theory and then later as…what exactly? An investor? No, it was more than that. He'd gotten his hands dirty and they'd worked together. It felt good and she missed sharing it with him now. Missed more than that, too. Missed his teasing smile and sparkling eyes. Missed the way he moved and the sound of his voice. No doubt about it, she still had it bad.

The days passed by and still no sign of Clay. Meg ignored his orders to not work and defiantly finished the fence and constructed the picnic tables. She followed doctor's orders and went for a massage and booked an appointment to have her edema assessed. The hayfields turned green and began to grow tall as the month of May progressed. Dawson was out with Tara more often than not and Meg sat home alone. Even if they constantly butted heads, she missed Clay and she didn't like the way they'd left things.

Finally, as the holiday weekend approached, Meg had to do something about it. After dinner, when Dawson was headed out to meet Tara yet again, Meg walked over to Clay's with the chirpy sound of the peepers and the newborn scent of spring urging her along.

She found him beneath the mower, laying on an old piece of cardboard to keep him off of the damp earth. His shirtsleeves were rolled up past the elbows revealing strong, tanned forearms. His jeans were dirty and his boots scuffed.

She shouldn't have found him so desperately attractive, but she did.

"Tuning up for first cut?"

She could see his face through the spaces, the shadows on his cheekbones as the mellowing sun was blocked by the mower discs. His eyes showed surprise, then relief, and then she watched, intrigued, as both emotions were shuttered away and he turned his attention back to the mower.

"You're feeling better," he replied.

She gave his foot a nudge with her own. "I've been feeling better for weeks."

He didn't answer and Meg was truly afraid now. Were things ruined between them for good? He was acting like he didn't care at all. At least before he'd cared enough to give her a hard time. His parting words echoed in her ears. "Love? Who said anything about love?" Maybe he wasn't in love with her, but she refused to believe he didn't care at all. That their friendship meant nothing.

She took a breath, determined to get him to talk. They had to clear the air somehow. She had to try. They were both stubborn and proud, but she'd sacrifice a bit of that to fix things.

"Since you haven't been policing my activity, I guess you decided not to enforce your ultimatum?"

He slid out from beneath the mower, his body making a shushing sound along the cardboard. He got up, put his tools in his toolbox and latched the lid. "It would take a freight train to stop you from doing what you wanted. I thought I'd save myself the time and pain of beating my head against a wall."

He picked up the toolbox.

Meg couldn't help the hurt that pierced her heart. She was trying, and he was so cold. He'd put a wall around himself and seemed determined to keep it in place, shutting her out. "What did you expect me to do," she whispered. "Say woe is me and give up? I don't know how to do that."

She didn't want to give up on him, either. Their relationship, if it could be called that, was muddled and messy. But she didn't want it to be over. She wanted Clay in her life. In what capacity she still didn't know, but no Clay at all was inconceivable.

"I know," he conceded. For a long moment he looked at her and she felt small. She hated feeling that somehow she'd disappointed him, let him down. At the same time the awareness she knew neither of them liked prickled along the back of her neck. His words came back to taunt her: *Not as over as we thought, then.* It gave her courage.

"Can we talk? I can't go on this way, Clay."

He nodded. "Let me put this away."

Meg waited for him outside the house. The rosebushes were budding and he'd already turned the earth in preparation for a vegetable garden on the south-facing side. In a month or two everything would be green and fragrant. Right now it seemed like it was holding its breath, waiting for the right amount of sun and rain to make it flourish. Clay came walking across the lawn and Meg swallowed. He belonged here. This ranch, this house—it was a part of him and he was a part of it. She realized that her fledgling business was her way of seeking that sort of connection for herself. As he came closer, her heart thumped heavily. That deep-rooted belonging, the confidence in his place in the world was incredibly sexy. She might as well admit it—there would always be a part of her that was drawn to Clay Gregory.

Once inside he took off his boots and she pushed off her sneakers with her toes, leaving them by the door. He offered her a drink and she declined. The sun was beginning to go down and the light came through the windows of the kitchen, soaking the room in a yellowy glow. Nerves twisted her stomach into knots. She wished she knew how to begin. What to say. And the longer the silence drew out, the more difficult it became.

Clay put his hand on the back of a chair, and she watched, transfixed, as he lifted his head, squared his shoulders and turned to face her. His hands were dirty from working on the machinery and a stripe of brown swiped across the front of his shirt, drawing her gaze to the firm muscle beneath the fabric. Her breath seemed to lodge in her lungs as she lifted her gaze to his.

The moment their eyes made contact, something snapped. Clay stepped forward and without any prelude or finesse, pulled her close against his rock-hard body and kissed her.

Not the seductive, melting kisses that had produced a slow burn that night in her foyer. Meg's body kicked into overdrive at the effect of Clay, unleashed. His mouth slanted relentlessly over hers and she responded, gasping as he lifted her clean off the floor and deposited her on the countertop like she weighed nothing at all. Her legs wrapped around him and she felt the way their bodies matched up, reveling in the sheer physicality of it. Oh, my glory, she thought. There wasn't a single part of him that wasn't hard and muscled. And then any thoughts that would have followed were swept away as his mouth slid from hers and he nibbled on her earlobe, sending a jolt of electricity straight to her core.

His mouth gentled, lightly nipping and kissing her neck, jaw, lips. Meg lifted her arms and looped them around his neck, twining her fingers in the rich thickness of his dark hair. Her eyes closed and she dropped her head back as he dropped a kiss on her chin. "I thought you hated me," she murmured, and then sighed as he slid his fingers over the column of her neck.

"Fear," he murmured back. "Fear and anger, but not hate, Megan. Never hate."

She opened her eyes. Her body seemed to be pulsing everywhere and it was in contact with his in several places. She tightened her legs, holding him against her, wanting to be even closer. Craving it. "What are we doing, Clay?" The words hung in the air, heavy with suggestion.

"I don't know," he admitted. His eyes glowed nearly black in the mellow light, holding a dangerous, sexy edge of promise. "But I don't want to stop."

But how far could they take this? Meg thrilled when he kissed her again, but the warning was beginning to beat in her head. When Clay's hands began to roam, she reached for his wrists as the familiar panic rushed into her veins.

"I can't," she whispered, and then hated herself for it. Hated that she said it, hated how her body looked. Hated that she wished for something she could never have—her perfectly shaped, whole body back.

She thought he would step away, but he didn't. He twisted his wrists so that they slipped from her grasp and then held her fingers within his own, squeezing them reassuringly. "I stayed away," he said softly, "because I knew this would happen, and I knew you weren't ready. I wanted to give you time." He sighed, and when he looked at her this time she thought she saw sadness soften his eyes. "But I don't think time is enough to fix this, is it?"

She was so afraid. Of moving forward, of losing Clay forever. "What do you want, Clay? You think you want something but you don't really know. You've conveniently glossed over the reality that is me. You think that this time is different, right? Your mom left but you're not like her. We both know that.

"But you don't know what you're asking. You don't really know because you haven't seen. You don't know because you've never sat in the doctor's office and heard the diagnosis. You couldn't even handle a simple virus without losing it. Hearing truly bad news is a million times worse. If you looked…really looked at it, at me, at the disfigurement, you'd be gone. And, God help me, I don't want to lose you."

"So what happens? We stay this way forever? More than friends but not lovers? Kissing but never making love?"

The words sent a shiver over her.

"Because I do want to make love, Meg. I've wanted to since the wedding, and I'm tired of fighting it."

For one tempting, temporary moment she indulged in the fantasy. Clay's eyes glowed at her, his hard, muscled body within her reach. All she had to do was touch and he could be hers. But the fantasy was interrupted—as it always was—by the reality she couldn't escape.

"I can't go on that way," he said flatly. "And you can't, either." He stepped away from her and she missed the heat of his body nestled against hers. "It isn't fair to either of us."

Was this how it would be her whole life? A half existence, with one foot in and one foot out? And if she did take the risk, she'd be opening herself up to too much. As much as she wanted to believe he would be there for her, always, she couldn't quite buy into it. She had to let it go.

"I want you, Meg. I I—"

"No." She cut off the word before he could form it. She couldn't bear to hear him say the words and then lose him later, as she surely would. He wasn't thinking clearly. Never mind her scars. There'd be a spot on an X-ray or a change in her blood work and it would be too much for him to handle. Then where would she be? "We need to end this, now. It is not what you think, Clay. And you can't ride in on your steed and rescue me and pretend it's all better forever."

"That's not my intention."

"You don't want me. You want the idea of me. But you can't buy guarantees, Clay. You can't control the future. You want to save me like you couldn't save your dad."

He stepped back as she flung the words at him.

"You're right. I couldn't save my dad, no matter how I tried. But you're wrong that I want to save you instead. You want to know why this has been such a mess? Because I know that no matter what I do I *can't* save you, Meg. I'm helpless. It was easier to keep my distance, tell myself that if we were just friends I could still handle it. But I was wrong about that, too."

She hopped down from the counter; she felt way too exposed up there. "I'm sorry, Clay. I didn't come here to fight. I came to put our friendship back together. But it doesn't seem to be working. We always argue."

"Why do you think that is?" he asked. He put his hands in his pockets and the movement made his shoulders raise and lower. She was constantly aware of his physicality. He was so perfect. And she was not. She never would be.

What would it take to make him understand? The answer came to her instantly and she recoiled. No. She couldn't show him, couldn't make herself that vulnerable.

But logic nagged at her. If he wanted more, eventually they would come to this crossroad. She could talk until she was blue in the face but until he truly saw the evidence, he had his mind made up. It was time to get off the merry-go-round. She could do this. She had gone through worse times and come through. And maybe then they could stop this dance they were doing and find some level ground where they could salvage their friendship. At the rate they were going there would be nothing left but the ashes, and it was impossible to think of her world with no Clay in it.

She reached for the top button of her blouse.

"Meg, you don't have to…"

"Yes," she replied gently, "I do. This is what keeps this horrible push and pull thing going on. Let's just get it over with, Clay."

Clay's gaze never left hers as one by one she undid the buttons. When the last one was gone, she shrugged out of the shirt and let it drop to the floor. She took a shaky breath. This should have been a moment filled with anticipation and desire and the difference nearly broke her heart. All she felt was dread and self-loathing.

With shaking fingers, she reached behind her back, undid her bra and let it slide down her arms until it joined her blouse on the kitchen floor.

Clay swallowed against the lump that lodged in his throat. The backs of his eyes burned but he would not cry. Not when Megan was in front of him, being so very strong. Not when she trusted him this much. He loved her. She wouldn't let him say the words but it was true. He could see through her plan. She was trying to shock him into leaving so they wouldn't have to deal with what was between them. She was scared, too.

His gaze left hers and dropped, as they both knew it would. A hole seemed to open up in his core at the sight of her. One breast, pert and rosy-tipped, as natural as a warm spring rain. And her right side—flat, with a scar running from where her breast had been toward her arm-pit. The redness had healed long ago, but not so long as to make the scar invisible. It stood out clearly against the paleness of her skin.

He looked up into her face and saw the tears streaking down her cheeks, even though she'd never moved during his visual examination. Her eyes clashed with his, flared with defiance. By God, she was something. He'd called her obstinate, pigheaded, and even blind, but he'd missed out on something. Brave. Right now, faced with what he knew was horribly transparent and painful, she refused to cower.

She bent to reach for her bra and Clay stepped forward, putting his hand on her arm. Her head snapped up in alarm.

"Don't," he said roughly. It sounded too loud in the quiet kitchen. "Don't hide, please."

She straightened, but this time he noticed her shoulders hunched a little, like she was trying to shelter herself. He reminded himself to be gentle. She was expecting him to turn away. He moved his thumb and wiped away the tears that hung on her lashes. "Don't cry," he murmured. "My beautiful girl, don't cry."

Her lower lip quivered and he watched, intrigued, as she bit down on it.

Clay hadn't known what to expect. He'd checked Google for pictures to try to understand, to prepare himself, but it was different because it was Meg. She was not a cold, clinical photograph. She was flesh and blood, before him now, and the changes wrought on her body didn't make him want her any less.

As gently as he possibly could, he let his fingers trail down her neck. He felt her tremble beneath his finger-tips and forced himself to go painfully slow. He curled his fingers, letting them ride with a featherlight touch over the full curve of her breast. He met her gaze, making sure everything was all right, and was startled to see her pupils widen and her cheeks flush. Silently he asked permission. She held herself as rigid as a statue, her breath barely moving her chest as he took those same fingers and traced the line of her scar. Not quite as soft as the rest. Strong and tough. A warrior's mark. His heart pounding, he pressed his palm against the skin where her breast should have been.

Meg wasn't sure how much longer she could hold on to the thin thread of control. It had been torture standing before him, watching his gaze sweep down to stare at her mark. She'd nearly covered her healthy breast out of embarrassment, but she'd clenched her hands at her sides, determined he see it all. If they were suddenly talking about sex and love there was no room for false modesty. So she'd steeled herself for his revulsion, prayed for a quick end to the examination and a swift return to common sense.

Only it never came, and the longer he looked the more it tore her apart.

Now he was touching her and she was really fighting to keep from losing it. His fingers grazed her breast and she felt her body betray her, terrifying her with the intensity of her reaction. This wasn't how it was supposed to happen. It was supposed to be less, not more. Not this much more.

His fingers traced along the curved scar and then he pressed his palm against the spot where her breast had been. She felt the pressure of his hand, but the skin was numb. The soft, feathery sensations from the other side were absent here, and Meg wondered if she'd stopped feeling the same way the nerves in her chest wall had.

"I can't feel it," she whispered, closing her eyes. "I want to. I can imagine it. But I can't feel it, Clay."

"It doesn't matter. You're so beautiful, Meg. So brave."

But she wasn't. She wasn't beautiful, and as far as bravery, well it was all an act that she'd been keeping up for months. She shook her head, but he stopped her with the husky timbre of his voice. "I love you, Meg."

He folded her into his arms and Meg felt the rough fabric of his shirt against her skin, the warmth of his hands splayed across her naked back. Clay had just said he loved her. The world seemed to shrink into a microcosm of this moment where it was just the two of them and everything else was shut outside. His breath was warm against her hair, his lips soft as he kissed just above her ear. Not a kiss of passion, but more. A forever kind of kiss and Meg felt her heart turn over.

She couldn't say the words back; not because she didn't want to, but because it was too much to process in a short amount of time. She was still absorbing the sound of his declaration when he began kissing her again. Meg tried to give herself over to the sweetness of the sensation. Clay was a good man. *The* man, and he'd just said he loved her. She had expected a very different reaction from him just now and she should be happy. What on earth was her problem? She ignored the uneasy feeling, closed her eyes and sank into the kiss, reached for his shirt buttons and began unbuttoning them. With his lips still fused to hers he pulled his arms out of the sleeves and pulled her close, skin to skin. Meg's heart pounded as panic started to set in. She tried to ignore it, but when he scooped her up in his arms she lost her tenuous grip on her fears.

"Put me down." He started to walk toward the hall

that led to the bedrooms at the back of the house. "Clay! Stop. Please." Her breath caught on a sob. He released his arm and she slid slowly down until her feet hit the floor. Her bra and shirt were several feet away now and she felt horribly exposed. She crossed an arm over her chest.

"I can't do this. I thought I could, but I can't."

"I rushed you," he said, his gaze tender and understanding. "It's okay, Meg, we can take it slow…"

Oh, God, he was making it even worse than it already was. He had to stop being so patient, so understanding. Because she was beginning to see a glimmer of the real truth and she had to get out of here before he pushed too far.

"No," she answered. She had to stop trembling. "I didn't come here for this. I came here to salvage our friendship. I *can't*, Clay."

"There's more than friendship between us. How can you deny it?"

He raised his hand to cup her face and she backed away. It seemed a short time ago that he'd thrown love in her face and she'd been so hurt. Now their positions were reversed and she had to add regret to all the emotions churning within her. "I don't want this," she said, momentarily impressed at how clearly it came out. She had thought that revealing her scars was her biggest fear, but she'd been horribly wrong. She'd thought that Clay's past would get in their way and she'd been mistaken about that, too.

No, he'd been the one who was right all along. She was the one standing in their way. He might love her now but she'd loved him longest. And if they did this—made love, began a real relationship…

For all her brave and optimistic talk, she knew the deep down, ugly truth. She was petrified of her cancer coming back. And if she willingly entered into a romance with Clay, that might mean having him and then losing him, breaking her heart. She wanted to believe he'd stand by her, but it was a lot to expect. She knew the statistics. Knew what reoccurrence could mean. Even if he did stay…

It wasn't a big stretch to envision the eventual outcome. And then where would Clay be? Alone. How could she ask that of him when cancer had already extracted such a heavy price?

It had to end now, while they could still both recover. She wanted more for him. He deserved a whole woman and a long, happy life. He deserved someone to make this a home for him again and a brood of children running around. And she was terrified that she couldn't give that to him.

"No," she said, backing up and reaching for her shirt. In her haste to cover her body she put on her shirt and jammed her bra into a ball, clenching it in her white fingers.

"I'm sorry, Clay." His face had paled and she knew she'd remember his hurt expression as long as she lived. "I'm so damned sorry. I can't love you."

"Meg!" He stepped toward her, but she backed off. She couldn't let him touch her now. She was too fragile, she wanted what he was offering too much.

"I can't, Clay. You should just forget about me."

"Never."

Meg's eyes stung. Oh, why did he have to suddenly want to fight for them? Why couldn't he let her go as he always had before?

"Goodbye," she whispered. "Please don't follow me."

She left him standing in the kitchen.

CHAPTER ELEVEN

MEG tamped the stack of flyers together and slid them into a large envelope. Saturday was the grand opening and she was going to pop in to town this morning and deliver flyers to local businesses. Everything was ready—the barn and riding ring were finished and the extra insurance had been approved. She already had three boarders lined up and she'd bought two mild-mannered quarter horse mares from Brody Hamilton and was considering two more. Four summer day camps were scheduled and Megan hoped that registrations would begin to flow in after the weekend.

But somehow it felt empty. She looked down at her desk, set up in a corner of the small office her parents used for ranch business. One of the invitations she'd printed for a small group of personal friends remained on the top. Clay's. She knew he needed to be here. Despite their problems, he'd given her such a precious gift. If it weren't for him, the school would still be a pipe dream.

But she hadn't seen him since the night in his kitchen. They'd both been busy, but in all the years they'd known each other, they'd always run into each other occasionally. To go this long without so much as a sign of him meant he was avoiding her. Just as she was avoiding him.

There was a knock on the office door and Meg looked

up. Jen Laramie stood in the breach, holding out a tray of iced cinnamon buns and flashing a crooked smile.

Meg forced a bright smile. "Your timing is perfect."

"Isn't it always?"

Meg admired the fact that nothing ever managed to drag Jen down. She pushed her chair back and got up. "I could use a distraction." She knew she'd been hiding away too long, letting this thing with her and Clay make her blue. She had so much to be thankful for, to be happy about and it was time she pulled herself out of her funk.

"Mom put some decaf on before she left. I'll get the cream if you get plates."

In moments they were seated at the table with steaming mugs and sticky fingers. "Seen Clay lately?" Jen asked, a little too innocently. Meg knew everyone had seen them leave the wedding together, and that had only been a while ago. And Meg was sure that even though they'd never made their business agreement public, people were probably aware that Clay had bankrolled Meg's project. If there *hadn't* been some speculation, Meg would have been surprised.

"Not lately," she answered, focusing on a dribble of icing running down the side of her roll.

"Hmm. No one's seen much of him. Hasn't been to wing night in weeks. Neither of you have."

Did Jen think that she and Clay had been holed up together? Meg picked at a layer of pastry, wondering how to reply to the thinly veiled insinuation. So she wasn't the only one hiding out. It hurt her to know that she'd hurt him. That he'd never know how much she appreciated what he'd done for her. It wasn't just the loan. It was how she saw herself. His acceptance had changed so much.

And yet she still felt she'd done the right thing. This could all change in the blink of an eye. She wouldn't risk hurting him further. "I've been busy here," Meg said, taking a sip of coffee and keeping her face perfectly neutral. "And I'm sure Clay must be busy at his place, with haying starting and all."

Jen broke off a piece of pastry and popped it in her mouth. "Shoot, everyone's busy. We kind of thought maybe Clay was here helping you get set up."

"No," Meg answered simply. But the truth was, his absence stung. She had been the one to end things. It didn't make it easier, but she owned it. This time there was no ambiguity. It was over. And one day she'd be over Clay and it would be fine.

Jen leaned forward and studied Meg's face. "Girl, what's going on? Have you been sleeping?"

Meg forced a light laugh. She knew there were shadows under her eyes and knew what had put them there. "Are you kidding? I've been putting in long days, that's all. I fall into bed at night and sleep like a house fell on me."

She didn't say that she pushed so hard to try to forget Clay. That she welcomed the exhaustion so that she wouldn't lie awake in bed thinking about what she'd given up.

"Then you're unhappy." Jen leaned back and rested her fingers on her rounded belly as she frowned. Meg tried not to watch the way Jen's palm smoothed her maternity shirt out of habit. Meg had been right to walk away from Clay, hadn't she? He was the kind of man who needed a family, a son or daughter to take over the legacy he was building. Meg's treatment had been aggressive. Even if they might have made it past the physical issues, Meg didn't even know if she could get pregnant. It was just one more thing on the list, and Clay didn't even realize.

A lump lodged in her throat. She'd never thought about

it much before but she did want children. Especially little black-haired boys with irresistible eyes. Another thing on the list, yes. Another thing that set off the wistful longing she couldn't seem to escape lately, too. She'd asked Clay not to follow her and he hadn't. She'd blown any chance with him now, his continued absence told her that.

"Meg?"

She lifted her head, suddenly aware that she'd been staring into her coffee cup for too long. "Sorry, Jen."

"What happened between you?"

Meg shook her head. What had happened was between her and Clay.

"After the wedding, everyone thought…"

Meg got up from the table and collected their plates. "They thought wrong."

Jen waited for a minute, but then got up and followed Meg to the sink. Meg felt her friend's hands on her shoulders. She should be happy at this moment—her dream of her own business was coming true. Instead all she was feeling was sadness.

"If there was something between us, Jen, there's not now. I wanted to preserve our friendship, but after the last time…"

"The last time what?"

Meg thought back to all the hurtful things she'd said. Even though they were true, saying them had torn her apart. "The last time I saw Clay. We haven't spoken since. I hurt him, Jen. It was the last thing I wanted to do, but I know I hurt him. And now I'm such a coward I can't even bring myself to invite him on Saturday."

There. She'd admitted it. She was a complete chicken. She knew he deserved to be here but she wasn't at all confident about how she'd handle seeing him again, especially in a crowd.

Jen turned her around by the shoulders. "You should go apologize."

"It's too late for that."

Jen's mouth took on a determined shape and she looked Meg dead in the eye. "It's never too late to say you're sorry. For heaven's sake, Meg. We've all been there for each other for years. Clay loves you."

"I know."

Meg saw Jen's face light up. "Well then!"

"It's not that simple, Jen. Please...don't say anything. It's complicated."

"It's always complicated," Jen said wisely.

Wasn't that the truth. Meg knew Jen was right. Heavens, her road back to Andrew had been fraught with difficulty. Meg tried a smile. "Are married women always so wise?" she asked.

"Everyone has scars, Meg. It's not easy moving past them, especially when you don't want to get hurt again."

Meg's lips dropped open. "How did you know? I mean, is it that obvious?"

Jen's gaze softened. "Oh, honey, you're dealing with both kinds of scars—literal and figurative. You don't give Clay enough credit. Your mastectomy won't turn him away. And you can always go for reconstruction later, you know?"

"It's not that, not anymore," Meg replied. How things had changed since the day she went shopping for a dress in Lily's store. She was nowhere near as self-conscious as she had been. She went back to the table and sat, and Jen followed. Meg rested her forearms on the table. "I'm afraid, Jen. It's me, all me. You talk to all these survivors and it's like they have a new lease on life and they're so happy. And at times it's like that. Look at how I built this business. I'm *here*, and that's a victory in itself. But underneath it's hard, because I know what it's like. And I know how it feels to think for just a moment that you might not make it. And that gets me every time."

Jen didn't answer for a few minutes, but finally she looked up. "Then you have to decide which is more important. A life with Clay, or playing it safe."

She made it sound so easy when it wasn't. "It doesn't matter now anyway. It's over." She felt miserable as she met Jen's gaze. "Any other time he's come back. But not this time."

"Then you have to give him a reason to. I can't tell you what to do, Meg, but letting it fester won't help. You can't spend the rest of your life avoiding someone who only lives a mile away. Who is best friends with your brother."

"Then what do I do?"

Jen smiled. "You invite him to the grand opening. You smile. As far as the rest, you have to figure that out. But I want you to remember that I'm here, Meg. Anytime you need me. Lily, too. I know you might not be comfortable talking to Noah about your particular situation, but I know he'd understand. So many of us have always only wanted to help."

"I know." Meg's heart filled with gratitude and a bittersweet sort of love. "You all stuck by me even when I pushed you away."

Jen patted her hand. "Then maybe you won't be so silly again, hmm?"

It was time she accepted help. Time she let people in, she realized. Maybe Clay had been right, too. Maybe the only person demanding perfection was her.

Meg thought back to the invitation on her desk. If Jen was so keen on helping, she'd surely run a tiny errand. "There is one thing you could do for me. Deliver his invitation. He's responsible for this happening and he should be here. I'm not sure he'd even accept it from me. But he will from you."

"You know I'll do anything I can."

Meg went to the office and got the invitation along with a handful of flyers. "If you can pass these out at Snickerdoodles, that'd be great." She smiled at Jen. Even as she got nearer to her due date, Jen had an energy about her that Meg admired. It was happiness, Meg realized with a spurt of envy. The feeling soon went away. She would never begrudge anyone a chance at happiness. It was her own dissatisfaction talking. Besides, talking to Jen had somehow lifted part of the weight that seemed to drag her down lately. Perhaps the old saying was right after all—a burden shared was a burden halved.

"You've done so much already. Offering to provide the food for the Open House means so much. I don't deserve it."

"Don't be silly. That's what friends are for."

Meg knew she was right. That everyone had been right all along. In this town—in this circle—people looked out for each other. Meg had felt so much love and acceptance since her return. But it had made her feel like she had very little to offer back. Maybe it was time she tried to change that.

"Either way, I want you to know I appreciate your support."

"I'll drop this off in Clay's mailbox before I go back to town."

Meg gave Jen an impulsive hug. "Thank you," she murmured. "For everything. I feel so much better."

Jen gave her a squeeze and stepped back. "Don't give up yet," she said with a wink. "And I'll see you Saturday."

When Jen was gone Meg wandered back to the office. She picked up the striped rock that she used as a paperweight these days. It served as a reminder of her years of friendship with Clay and what he'd sacrificed to make this Saturday possible. She hoped that someday they could find their way back to that friendship, but she wasn't too optimistic. There would never be that open, easy way between them again. Once you loved someone, things changed. Wounds of the heart didn't heal with a few sutures and time.

The rock warmed in her hand and she closed her eyes. She wished so many things could be different. Most of all she wished she had what it took to make him happy. Maybe setting him free was the best way to do that. Which was fine—for Clay.

But Meg knew she wouldn't be free. And the alternative that stretched before her was a lifetime of being alone.

She put down the rock, dissatisfied. Somehow it didn't seem like much of an alternative at all.

The last thing Clay wanted to do on a Saturday evening was go to the Briggs ranch. He'd put if off as long as he could. The invitation Jen had delivered said four o'clock until nine. It was already past seven.

He put his foot up on the bench and gave his boots a final rub of the cloth. She hadn't even delivered the invitation herself and that spoke volumes. Was she so desperate to avoid his company? He had put himself out there, laid his heart on the line and she'd handed it back to him saying she couldn't love him. He'd stayed away not out of anger but because he knew she was hurting, and he had no desire to make it harder for her.

But he had to go. No matter what had happened between him and Meg, he knew how it would look if he stayed away. Everyone knew he'd loaned her the money. And the Briggs family was too important to him. His absence would be noted, and he couldn't avoid Meg forever. So he'd go to her grand opening and smile and nod at the new stable extension and ring and then he'd come home. He had no desire to ruin her big day.

To kill more time, he walked the mile between their houses.

It was seven-thirty when he arrived and the yard was full of vehicles. Country music played from a sound system somewhere and voices were raised in laughter and conversation. Three long tables were set up with quickly diminishing platters of food and washtubs contained melting ice and canned drinks. In the center of the garden was a new sign: Mountain View Stables. Red geraniums and white petunias blossomed in the surrounding bed and the picnic tables Meg had built were full of neighbors and friends. Clay moved past them and into the barn out of the noise. He hadn't seen Meg anywhere, but he was sure she was basking in the glory of the moment. The place looked like a total success.

He was happy for her. He was glad he'd helped. But he was still bitter about how things had ended up. He'd offered her everything—his love—and she'd handed it right back to him.

Dawson came out of the tack room with Tara just as Clay turned the corner. Tara blushed and Dawson wore a foolish grin. "Hey," he said to Clay, keeping Tara close to his side. "Glad you finally made it."

Dawson's face was cheerful but Clay heard the underlying steel in the words. He should have come earlier and made an early excuse to depart. Irritation that had been bubbling all day flared. Dawson was going to play big brother when he knew nothing of the situation. He would

blame Clay when it had been Meg who told him to leave
her alone. He didn't even know what Dawson's problem
was. He had nothing to fear from Clay. It was over. "Just
finishing up some haying," he said lightly, knowing it
sounded lame. "This was the first I could get away."

Tara looked up at Dawson, then back at Clay. "I think
I'll go get a drink." She moved out of Dawson's embrace
but Clay heard her whisper, "Be nice," as she left.

Clay studied his friend. His best friend. Since this
whole thing had begun with Megan things had been tense
between them, as he always knew it would be. Ever since
the wedding he'd felt Dawson's watchful eye. Dating a
friend's sister was problematic—Dawson had no idea
exactly how problematic. Clay didn't want to get into it
so he deliberately deflected. "Things are getting pretty
serious between you and Tara."

"You could say that. Not so serious between you and
my sister, though, right?"

It felt like a challenge and Clay was just frustrated
enough to be annoyed that Dawson wouldn't take the
hint. "Maybe you should ask Meg about that."

"I'm asking you."

What a time for Dawson to start playing the protective
big brother. Clay clenched his teeth. "You don't have to
worry about me making a move on your sister, okay?"

Dawson took a step forward. "I warned you about hurting her." Dawson frowned. "Now she's moping through
the house and you're nowhere to be found. It doesn't take
a genius to figure it out. Damn it, Clay, I should kick
your…"

"Do it, then," Clay suggested, feeling his temper smol-
der. "Just do it if it will make you feel better."

Dawson's steely gaze tempered. "I can't do that."

"Why not?"

"Because I don't think she's the only one hurting."

Clay met Dawson's gaze evenly. Wasn't this a fine turnaround? And the timing for pushing them together was perfect. Clay sighed. "You really should talk to Meg, bro. Though if you wanted to knock me around a bit I probably wouldn't stop you. I can't possibly feel any worse."

Dawson's body relaxed. "You love her then."

Clay considered lying and then figured there was no point. He'd counted on Dawson taking Meg's side, he realized. Knowing her brother, his friend, was trying to fix things between them only made the cut that much deeper.

"Of course I love her, you idiot. But it's not all up to me."

"Did you tell her?"

"Frankly that's none of your business."

Dawson shook his head and leaned back on the stall door. "What a pair you make. Jen said Meg's being as stubborn as you are and she's been moping around the house for days. Meg wouldn't even deliver your invitation for today. Neither of you have come out to the pub in weeks and don't say you're too busy. You're no more busy than the rest of us, and we've *all* noticed you dancing circles around each other. I don't know what happened, and—" he gave Clay a dark look "—I don't think I want to. But you guys need to talk. This is crazy."

"Leave it alone, Dawson. Not tonight, not during her big night."

"But…"

"Don't you get it? I don't want to talk to her right now."

Clay heard a choked sound to his left and looked up. Meg was standing there, her dark eyes enormous and shining with tears. For a flash, a current seemed to run between them, the same buzz he felt every time she

looked at him. Would it always be this way? This jolt of
electricity? The sizzling attraction? This was why he'd
avoided her. It was too hard to love her and have this distance between them.

She'd heard what he'd just said, he was sure of it, and
had completely misinterpreted it out of context. Damn
it, was nothing going to go right tonight? He should have
followed his first instinct when the invitation had landed
in his mailbox—stayed home.

"Meg, I..."

Loud voices sounded by the barn entrance, coming
closer and Meg's eyes widened further with alarm. She
wouldn't want anyone to see her upset, and he ignored
Dawson and rushed forward. Before she could even voice
a protest, he grabbed her hand and hauled her into the
tack room that Dawson and Tara had just vacated. "I'm
locking the door," Clay advised Dawson in an undertone.
"You make sure we have some privacy."

Clay shut the door and latched the hook. The room
was a good size, but the abundance of tack and supplies
made it feel smaller, closed in. It smelled of leather and
the musty but pleasant scent of blankets. Clay looked at
Meg and felt his heart take a leap. "You look beautiful,"
he said quietly. She wore a Western style dress in pink, of
all things, with a belt slung over her hips and new boots.
The hue set off the roses in her cheeks, and he noticed
that her hair had grown more, curling out at the tips in
a soft, feminine look. The weeks of avoiding her hadn't
helped at all. "I don't think I've ever seen you in pink
before."

"The pink is for..."

"I know," he said gently. These days the color pink was
automatically associated with breast cancer awareness.

"I have to stop hiding behind it," she said quietly. "I can't pretend it didn't happen. That it didn't change me."

Clay swallowed. It had changed her in more ways than she knew. He'd loved the old Meg but he hadn't been in love with her the same way he was now. He'd relied on her but he hadn't been the strong man she deserved. That ended now. He still loved her. Still wanted her.

He still wanted it all. Still believed in her.

And she was still looking at him like he couldn't be trusted.

Meg watched Clay run a hand over his face. When she'd invited him she hadn't envisioned them being locked in a tack room together. She'd rather thought he'd come, look around, shoot the breeze with Andrew and Noah and Dawson and stay out of her way.

As the hours had ticked by, she'd convinced herself he wasn't coming and tried to push away the disappointment. She told herself he'd rejected her invitation and her the way she'd asked him to. She blinked. Asked? No, she'd demanded he leave her alone and he'd done just that.

Seeing him with Dawson had given her heart such a lurch she was certain he could hear it. And then she'd heard what he said and the words still rang in her ears— *I don't want to talk to her right now.*

She'd been successful then, in driving him away. In making him see reason. But she'd also been right. The friendship between them was destroyed. Things would never be the same. Their houses, their businesses would only be a mile apart but the distance between them in every other way was impossible to measure. How could she survive it, knowing how much she loved him?

But how could she not? His ranch was his life and she had built hers here. It was what she wanted, wasn't it? A

place of her own. Her own legacy, a life-affirming sym-
bol, a way to ease her family's burdens. She couldn't give
it up. Didn't want to give it up. For everything there was a
price, and the deterioration of her relationship with Clay
was hers.

"I'm fine, Clay. I should get back to the guests."

She squared her shoulders. She could do this. Took one
step, two. Couldn't look into his strong, beautiful face as
she passed by him to go to the door. And then his hand
grabbed her wrist.

"Don't go."

She stopped, fought for breath. Still couldn't meet his
gaze. She had to be strong. Nothing had changed. "I have
to. Please, let me go, Clay."

"I wish to God I could."

He dropped her wrist, but Meg couldn't move now. If
she walked away it would be forever and her feet refused
to listen to her brain. They'd hurt each other so badly.
She dropped her chin. "Why are you making this so difficult? Why can't you just understand what I was saying
and leave it at that?"

Why couldn't they just stop caring about each other?

"I've tried," he whispered hoarsely. "Lord knows I've
tried."

"You can let me go," she whispered back. "You have
to put your foolish ideas out of your mind. I'm not the
girl for you. You'll see I'm right one day."

"So what are you going to do, run again?"

"Again?" She looked at him then, as the two of them
stood shoulder to shoulder. There was no challenge in his
eyes, no anger or pain. Just acceptance. "What do you
mean, again?"

"You told me once that you would always be there for
me," he replied. "But you lied. Oh, I know, when you got

sick you didn't want to be a burden to those who loved you. When you came back, you kept everyone at arm's length. The moment I got close you pushed me away. And then things changed, Meg. I needed you. I told you I loved you and you couldn't leave fast enough. You accused me of being scared but it's not me, it's you now. Run, Megan. Run so you never have to face what's right in front of you. So you never have to care too much. You're good at it."

Meg's lips dropped open. "How dare you," she whispered. "How dare you judge me, when you don't know…"

"I tried to understand. I tried time and time again. You let me in, once." His gaze was steady on hers and made her feel very, very small. "You let me in once and what you saw scared you to…"

"To death," Meg answered. Clearly. Because that was what this was really about. "Say it. To death."

"I don't need to, not anymore," he replied. "But I think you might."

Meg moved away, as far as she could in the crowded room. She rested her hand on the horn of a new saddle. They were going to clear the air once and for all. Tonight. While business associates and clients and neighbors enjoyed free food and music and laughter, she and Clay were going to ground zero in their relationship. So be it.

"I'm very familiar with death," she said sharply. "More familiar than you can imagine."

"And it scares you. You faced it and won but you're not so sure you can again. You think I don't understand? Do you think it's been easy for me knowing there are no guarantees? At least I'm still here."

Anger flared in Meg's chest. "Well, bully for you. I'm sorry I'm not the perfect Clay Gregory who has made all the right choices. Do you have any flaws, Clay? Any weaknesses?"

He didn't reply, but the answer may have just as well been spoken since they both heard it. *She* was his weakness. How many times had she been tempted? The words were there waiting to be said. In would be so easy right now to just give in and pretend it was all okay. But Meg had been through the fire once before and she knew what it did to a person. And every time she thought about giving in, she felt the lick of those flames and knew she couldn't do that to him.

"When are you going to stop running?" he demanded.

She scrambled to make sense of things. Clay always opened up all these feelings she'd rather keep shuttered away. He kept pushing but not hearing her! "You don't listen," she said, letting go of the saddle horn. She folded her arms around her middle, trying to hold on to her emotions but they were bubbling way too close to the surface. "You don't get it. I'm not running anymore, Clay. If anything, I'm seeing things clearly. I see you. I really see you. And you need someone who can be there for you always. I can't give you that. You're right, okay?" Her voice lifted but she was unable to stop. "I *am* afraid to face it again. I *am* afraid that the next time I won't win. And if I don't win, that means I die. It means losing everything! You need more than that. You need someone who will be there forever. You need someone who can give you lots of babies and a happy house and...and security. I can't give you those things, Clay, and I want you to have them." Her voice was high and shaking now. "I can't make you happy! So please. Please, find someone else!"

Clay stepped forward. "There is no one else!" he yelled. The air in the room vibrated as the words rang out.

Then, to Meg's dismay, Clay dropped his head. "There is no one else."

Those words, quietly uttered, shredded her emotions more than any angry outburst. She felt like crying but knew it wouldn't help either of them. She'd never truly seen Clay defeated before, and if her heart hadn't been broken before, it was now. She had wanted to save him from pain, and all she'd done was destroy him.

Meg held her breath as Clay raised his head. His eyes glittered and everything in her melted. She hadn't seen Clay cry since the one time she'd caught him crying in the pasture after his mother's abandonment. He was right. She had promised him she would always be there for him but she hadn't kept her promise, because she had held herself back from loving him when he needed her most.

Not in all the years she'd known him had she seen him this emotionally naked. And it was because of her.

CHAPTER TWELVE

"Don't," she whispered. "Oh, Clay. I would give anything not to hurt you."

He let his gaze drop to her mouth, her beautiful, bow-shaped mouth that just now was quivering with emotion. He understood now and rather than ruin him he felt the glimmerings of hope. She was afraid, but afraid *for* him. It changed everything. He took another step closer and he could see the sheen of moisture sitting on her lower eyelids. If she blinked it would surely spill over on to her cheeks. But she didn't blink. He held her gaze, drawing her to him like a magnet. He lifted his hand and ran it down her arm until he clasped her hand in his.

"I went into this with my eyes wide open," he said. "I was so afraid, Meg. You'd always been there for me. It was easy with you and suddenly all that was gone. All the hateful things I said before you went to Calgary—they ate at me for months. I tried to get through to you and I failed. I thought of you alone, taking your treatment, and it nearly drove me out of my mind, wondering how you were. Yes, I was afraid. But not knowing was worse. The mind can think up horrible scenarios."

"I was afraid to let anyone see me that way."

"I know," he answered. "But I missed you. I missed seeing you all the time and laughing with you and I missed just knowing you were there." He squeezed her fingers. "I missed you," he repeated simply.

"I missed you, too. Thought about you when I was alone, wondered how you were, wished I could talk to you. But I knew it would be too hard for you…"

"So you tried to protect me, too," he murmured. How many times over the years had she tried to spare him from pain? How had he never seen what was right in front of him before—how much he loved her?

He rubbed his thumb along her wrist. "When you came back, I tried again. I told myself it was because there were years of friendship between us. I tried to ignore how I really felt because I was scared, Meg. I admit it. I watched my father die, and I watched it destroy my mother. She didn't just leave him, she left me. And I didn't ever want to give anyone the power to leave me again."

"This is exactly what I'm saying." Meg nodded, but Clay put a finger over her lips.

"Hush, and let me finish."

He slid his finger off her mouth, but his gaze dropped there just for a moment, almost like a kiss before he continued on.

"It didn't work. I fell in love with you, Meg. I knew it the night of the wedding. You were so beautiful. Transformed. I acted on impulse and kissed you but it changed everything. Suddenly you weren't just my friend anymore—you were so much more. I tried to back off. I wanted to protect my heart so I told myself that I'd be better off keeping my distance and so I decided to help you with this place instead."

He swept his hand out to the side. "And it's amazing. You've done it, and it's going to be wonderful. I'm so proud of you, Meg."

"I owe you so much, Clay, I know that."

"No, you don't. Because I didn't give it freely, you

see? I gave you this so I wouldn't have to give you my-self. I'm not proud of that, but I understand it now and I won't make the same mistake again."

He took her hand in his. "And then you got sick and I nearly went out of my mind with worry and worst case scenarios. It was then that I figured it out. It doesn't mat-ter how hard I try to keep my heart safe. It's already yours. I tried to show you that. Tried to tell you that it didn't matter. I love you as you are. I accept that you come with risks. I want you anyway. No matter what."

"And I keep pushing you away," she whispered.

"Because you're afraid. Because you think you're not enough. But you are, Meg. Because there is no one else for me but *you*. There never has been, not since the day when you were seven years old and you took my hand in yours and said you would always be there. Why do you think all my relationships ended after a few weeks? It just took me a long time to figure it out. I had to face losing you to realize that I don't want to give up. I don't want to walk away. Because if I do that, I have nothing."

Her lower lip quivered as she whispered, "I love you so much that the idea of having you and losing you again is paralyzing."

His heart soared as she finally said the words he'd wanted to hear for so long. So close. It was all within his reach now. "Say it again."

She swallowed, seemed to struggle with the words. Gorgeous girl, he knew it wasn't easy for her. But he'd wait. He'd wait forever if that was what it took to hear her say it again.

"I love you."

"Now believe in it."

He held out his arms.

* * *

She couldn't hold out any longer. In all the weeks, the months since she'd come home, she'd fought the need to walk into his embrace. With a sob she took the final step into his arms and the security and acceptance waiting. His arms tightened around her, holding her close. She wrapped hers around his ribs, spreading her hands over his shoulder blades. This was where she belonged. It was where she'd always belonged. How foolish she'd been to push it away.

For long moments they stood that way, holding on to each other. Something happened in those moments; a recognition that there was no more fighting feelings, no more fighting fate. That whatever was to come they'd face together. The muted sound of the music outside disappeared. Meg knew she should be out there to see people off. The business was what she'd worked toward for ages. But this…oh, this. This was far more important.

"Okay?" Clay finally spoke into the stillness, the word vibrating in his throat so that Meg felt it against her hair. She nodded, the stubble of his jaw rasping against the tender skin of her cheek. Nothing had ever felt so wonderful. It was okay. It was more than okay.

"I'm sorry," she murmured, lifting her hand and touching his face.

"No more sorry. No more hiding and running, Meg. Only love and trust and being there for each other from now on. You don't have to do this alone."

"Now I have you beside me," she replied with a wobbly smile. "I've loved you for so long, Clay."

"How long?"

She smiled. "A long time. Maybe since you gave me this." She put her hand in her skirt pocket and took out the rock.

"Good grief. You've kept that silly thing all this time?"

"Of course I did. I was eight years old and my hero gave it to me." She smiled up at him. "It's my good luck charm, you know. I had it with me the day you asked me to be your date at the wedding. Where all this started."

Clay stepped back a little and the air around her felt cold, until he knelt on the dusty floor of the tack room. "In that case…I probably should have waited. Taken you somewhere romantic and made it special, but I don't want to wait. I don't want us to waste a single moment, or piece of good luck." He held her hand in his. "Will you marry me, Meg?"

She had no idea what the future held. But then, who did? She had been afraid to reach out her hand to him, afraid that he would not take it. But he had taken it anyway. And now that he had, she didn't intend to let it go. Clay Gregory. Her childhood hero, friend and now lover.

But one barrier still stood in their way, one thing that Meg knew she had to be honest about to be utterly fair to him. "Before I answer, Clay, you need to know that it might be difficult for me to have children. It could take a long time, or not at all." She held her breath, hating the words, wishing she didn't have to say them. Now that happiness was so close, knowing she truly might not have children of her own felt very bitter indeed.

Clay got to his feet, the knee of his jeans dusty from the floor. He cupped her face in his hands, touched her lips with his, and smiled.

"Then that's how it is. If we want children, we will find a way, I promise. There's always adoption. Where would I be now if Aunt Stacy hadn't adopted me? Now," he said firmly, "do you have any other objections or are you ready to give me an answer?"

She loved the hint of a smile that flirted with his lips as he asked. "Yes," she answered, letting her heart fill with joy where once fear had lived. "My answer is yes," she repeated and gave a whoop when Clay lifted her in his arms and spun her in a jubilant circle.

November was usually known as a bleak, gray month, but to Meg it was the most glorious month of the year. The harvests were in, the first snows from the Rockies had given the prairie a dusting of white, and today she would marry Clay Gregory and start her new life. Downstairs the guests were waiting. Up here, in the biggest room of the Inn, Meg was soaking in every precious minute of the day she'd never thought she'd have.

Lily and Tara, dressed in bronze satin gowns, arranged Meg's train while Jen handed her a bouquet of warm-hued roses threaded with pearls. Only Meg and the florist knew that in the center of the arrangement was an oval rock with a golden streak through the middle. Meg reached out and took Jen's hand.

"Thank you," she said, then turned to look at Lily and Tara. "All of you. For being there for me, even when I made it difficult. For helping make today so special."

Jen stepped back and smiled. "You look gorgeous, Meg."

"So do you." Jen's dress was slightly different, the same rich bronze but featuring an empire waist similar to Meg's style. The latest member of the Laramie family, MacKenzie Gerald, was only twelve weeks old and Lily had worked her magic. The result was flattering styles for the bridesmaids and a stunning, flowing gown in ivory for Meg. The sheer overskirt was the most romantic thing Meg had ever seen.

There was a knock on the door. Jen's skirt made the shushing sound that only long gowns make as she went to the door and opened it a crack. She came back with a smile. "Two minutes. And Drew says Clay's as nervous as a long-tailed cat in a room full of rocking chairs. Direct quote."

Meg wanted to laugh but could barely breathe. The girls picked up their bouquets and lined up at the door to make their descent down the stairs, where they'd wait at the door for their cue. Meg clutched her bouquet and followed. Her father waited at the door, slightly stooped because of his back but beaming in a tuxedo complete with jeweled bolo tie.

"Dad."

"Sweetheart."

They started down the stairs but halfway down her father stopped and pressed his free hand to her arm.

"Meg, I'm not the kind of man who expresses his feelings very well, or often. But I want you to know. I'm real proud of you, honey. Your mom and I both are. How you took on your treatment and how you built your own business. Clay's a good man, but I made it clear to him he's getting the real prize."

"Dad." Meg was in true danger of ruining her makeup as she blinked rapidly. It was tantamount to a speech for her father. Not that she'd ever questioned his love. It had always just been there.

"I didn't tell you to make you cry. I just…" He cleared his throat. "Before I give you away to another, I want you to know that we have never considered you a burden." At Meg's startled look he smiled. "I may be a man of few words, but I see things, Meg. Having you as our daughter has been our privilege. Never a burden. Never forget how much we love you."

"Oh, Daddy." Meg sniffled and the congregated guests could wait. She wrapped her arms around his neck and gave him a hug.

He smiled. "Now, let's go get you married. You've kept Clay waiting long enough."

And she had, she realized. The summer and fall had seemed endless, even though she'd had the business to get off the ground and they both had ranches to run. Now their interests would be joined; she was still going to run the stable as part of the Briggs family business with Clay as her partner.

The music started and the doors opened.

Clay waited at the end of the aisle and the moment their gazes met everything else faded away. She didn't see the faces of their friends, or the glowing candles, or the stands of flower arrangements. She only saw Clay, so tall and dashing in his tuxedo sporting his own bolo and spit-shined new boots. Clay, who'd challenged her at every moment. Clay, who'd believed in her when everyone else considered her a risk. Clay, who'd been so very sure of her when she hadn't even been sure of herself. His lips began to curve and so did hers, until they were both smiling brilliantly at each other. She was no longer afraid. Instead she was looking forward to their future together, no matter what it held for them.

Her hand was placed inside his, warm and secure. And when the minister asked, her answer was as crystal as a bell.

"I do."

* * * * *

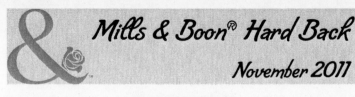

Mills & Boon® Hard Back
November 2011

ROMANCE

The Power of Vasilii	Penny Jordan
The Real Rio D'Aquila	Sandra Marton
A Shameful Consequence	Carol Marinelli
A Dangerous Infatuation	Chantelle Shaw
Kholodov's Last Mistress	Kate Hewitt
His Christmas Acquisition	Cathy Williams
The Argentine's Price	Maisey Yates
Captive but Forbidden	Lynn Raye Harris
On the First Night of Christmas...	Heidi Rice
The Power and the Glory	Kimberly Lang
How a Cowboy Stole Her Heart	Donna Alward
Tall, Dark, Texas Ranger	Patricia Thayer
The Secretary's Secret	Michelle Douglas
Rodeo Daddy	Soraya Lane
The Boy is Back in Town	Nina Harrington
Confessions of a Girl-Next-Door	Jackie Braun
Mistletoe, Midwife...Miracle Baby	Anne Fraser
Dynamite Doc or Christmas Dad?	Marion Lennox

HISTORICAL

The Lady Confesses	Carole Mortimer
The Dangerous Lord Darrington	Sarah Mallory
The Unconventional Maiden	June Francis
Her Battle-Scarred Knight	Meriel Fuller

MEDICAL ROMANCE™

The Child Who Rescued Christmas	Jessica Matthews
Firefighter With A Frozen Heart	Dianne Drake
How to Save a Marriage in a Million	Leonie Knight
Swallowbrook's Winter Bride	Abigail Gordon

1011 GEN STD HB

Mills & Boon® Large Print

November 2011

ROMANCE

HISTORICAL

MEDICAL ROMANCE™

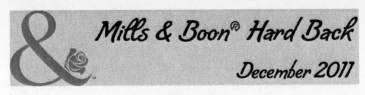

ROMANCE

Jewel in His Crown	Lynne Graham
The Man Every Woman Wants	Miranda Lee
Once a Ferrara Wife...	Sarah Morgan
Not Fit for a King?	Jane Porter
In Bed with a Stranger	India Grey
In a Storm of Scandal	Kim Lawrence
The Call of the Desert	Abby Green
Playing His Dangerous Game	Tina Duncan
How to Win the Dating War	Aimee Carson
Interview with the Daredevil	Nicola Marsh
Snowbound with Her Hero	Rebecca Winters
The Playboy's Gift	Teresa Carpenter
The Tycoon Who Healed Her Heart	Melissa James
Firefighter Under the Mistletoe	Melissa McClone
Flirting with Italian	Liz Fielding
The Inconvenient Laws of Attraction	Trish Wylie
The Night Before Christmas	Alison Roberts
Once a Good Girl...	Wendy S. Marcus

HISTORICAL

The Disappearing Duchess	Anne Herries
Improper Miss Darling	Gail Whitiker
Beauty and the Scarred Hero	Emily May
Butterfly Swords	Jeannie Lin

MEDICAL ROMANCE™

New Doc in Town	Meredith Webber
Orphan Under the Christmas Tree	Meredith Webber
Surgeon in a Wedding Dress	Sue MacKay
The Boy Who Made Them Love Again	Scarlet Wilson

Mills & Boon® Large Print

December 2011

ROMANCE

Bride for Real — Lynne Graham
From Dirt to Diamonds — Julia James
The Thorn in His Side — Kim Lawrence
Fiancée for One Night — Trish Morey
Australia's Maverick Millionaire — Margaret Way
Rescued by the Brooding Tycoon — Lucy Gordon
Swept Off Her Stilettos — Fiona Harper
Mr Right There All Along — Jackie Braun

HISTORICAL

Ravished by the Rake — Louise Allen
The Rake of Hollowhurst Castle — Elizabeth Beacon
Bought for the Harem — Anne Herries
Slave Princess — Juliet Landon

MEDICAL ROMANCE™

Flirting with the Society Doctor — Janice Lynn
When One Night Isn't Enough — Wendy S. Marcus
Melting the Argentine Doctor's Heart — Meredith Webber
Small Town Marriage Miracle — Jennifer Taylor
St Piran's: Prince on the Children's Ward — Sarah Morgan
Harry St Clair: Rogue or Doctor? — Fiona McArthur

Mills & Boon® Online

Discover more romance at
www.millsandboon.co.uk

- **FREE** online reads
- **Books** up to one
  month before shops
- **Browse our books**
  before you buy

...and much more!

For exclusive competitions and instant updates:

 Like us on **facebook.com/romancehq**

 Follow us on **twitter.com/millsandboonuk**

 Join us on **community.millsandboon.co.uk**

Visit us Online Sign up for our FREE eNewsletter at
www.millsandboon.co.uk

WEB/M&B/RTL4/HB

SFW